MW01608339

Elic C Cowley Typ

THE MADELEINE
MURDERS

An Inspector Henri Corbet Mystery

Elizabeth Cowley Tyler

MINERVA PRESS
LONDON
ATLANTA MONTREUX SYDNEY

THE MADELEINE MURDERS
Copyright © Elizabeth Cowley Tyler 1998

All Rights Reserved

No part of this book may be reproduced in any form
by photocopying or by any electronic or mechanical means,
including information storage or retrieval systems,
without permission in writing from both the copyright owner
and the publisher of this book.

ISBN 0 75410 025 1

First Published 1998 by
MINERVA PRESS
315–317 Regent Street
London W1R 7YB

2nd Impression 1998
3rd Impression 1999

Printed in Great Britain for Minerva Press

THE MADELEINE MURDERS

An Inspector Henri Corbet Mystery

To Proust, Stendhal, and Paris, the City of Light.

'Paris is still that monstrous marvel, that astonishing assemblage of movements, of machines, of thoughts, the city of a hundred thousand novels, the centre of the world.'

Ferragus *by Honoré de Balzac*

All characters and events in this book are fictional and any resemblance to actual places, events or persons, living or dead, is purely coincidental.

Acknowledgements

My sincere thanks to the many people who have helped me in this venture. I know there are some I won't have space to mention, and to them I extend my apologies.

Many thanks to James G. Berman for believing in Inspector Corbet and to Madame M. Hamon of the Sorbonne and M. Eustace Erwin of the Musée de la Renaissance for reading my manuscript for cultural accuracy.

Dr. Isabelle H. Naginski of Tufts University and Dr. Robert Frye of Regis College are two excellent professors of French literature whose courses at Harvard Extension have inspired me, and they have read my book in the context of the cultural and literary tradition. I am very grateful to my long-time friend, Eleanor Ellis, for her editorial acumen and for her wonderful suggestions for strengthening my plot.

One can never overestimate the value of the love and support of friends in any creative endeavour. My deepest gratitude goes to Kay Nelson, Nicola Phillips and Rona Troderman-King for their loving, non-judgmental support and indulgence. I thank my cat, Mimi, for her devotion and comfort.

Lest I forget old friends whose paths may have diverged from mine, I thank and remember Mary Carleton, Eileen Grossman, Don Kalick, Kevin Kain, Donald Nutting, Dorothy Robertson, Glenna Scott and Oliver Thayer.

Justices Edward Bennett, Elbert Tuttle, and Robert Barton have made my work in the Superior Court a pleasure and have appreciated and nurtured my grander visions.

Last, but by no means least, my heartfelt gratitude to Dr Malcolm Marsden of Elmira College, who taught me to read literature, to George Gutman of Middlebury College in Paris, who deepened my love of French history, and to Julia Child, who brought French cooking into the homes of a whole generation of Americans and without whom Inspector Corbet may never have been born.

Many years had elapsed during which nothing of Combray... had any existence for me, when one day in winter as I came home, my mother seeing that I was cold, offered me some tea, a thing I did not ordinarily take... I raised to my lips a spoonful of tea in which I had soaked a morsel of cake. No sooner had the warm liquid, and the crumbs with it, touched my palate than a shudder ran through my whole body... An exquisite pleasure had invaded my senses... Whence could it have come to me, this all-powerful joy?... And suddenly the memory returns. The taste was that of the little crumb of *madeleine* which on Sunday mornings at Combray... my aunt Léonie used to give me, dipping it first in her own cup of real or of lime-flower tea...

Swann's Way, by Marcel Proust

Chapter One

The long, lanky train stretched down the tracks at Bordeaux in the direction of Paris. Except for the figure of one tall, slim, slightly stooped man who headed with a quick, deliberate step toward the stairs leading to a car in the rear, the platform was empty. The man was dressed all in black and carried a cane and an attaché case. The wind tore at his long white hair, waving it around his head like a flag. He ducked down as he mounted the steps and resisted the efforts of the trainman to take his case while he boarded the train.

Once inside the car, he looked around and headed for the only seat which remained totally empty. He settled himself down into it. Just as the train started to move, he stood again to remove his long black coat, placing it on the seat along with his cane. Seated again, he reached into the attaché case, drew out a sheaf of papers and began to look through them.

When the train was out of the station, a vendor came around selling drinks. Upon hearing his approach, the man in black took a small package from his case and opened a napkin out of which he took some shell-shaped yellow cakes. He reached into his pocket, pulled out a small silver pillbox, and held it in his hand.

'Tea, please,' he said when the vendor came to him. He dropped two small tablets from the silver box into the hot liquid and bit into the lemon-coloured cake. When the tablets had dissolved in the tea, he took a long drink and began to look at his papers again.

As the train raced forward, the man suddenly grabbed at his throat, making a rasping sound. He gasped as though he were choking. His face became bright red, his eyes bulged. He struggled to breathe. He clutched at his throat as though trying to dislodge something. A high-pitched, pinched scream filled the car.

The conductor arrived, lifted the man out of his seat, and put his arms around his chest just under his ribcage. The effort to dislodge whatever was causing his distress was futile. The man continued to struggle for air, his body leaning on the conductor's arms. Eventually, he slid to the floor in a heap. As he did so, he pulled down with him the ream of loose papers. They scattered all over, landing on his slumped body. The conductor bent over and placed two fingers on the side of the man's neck.

'We'll have to stop at Poitiers,' he cried. 'This man is dead.'

Chapter Two

'Everyone has his Vichy.' Inspector Henri Corbet of the Paris Police leaned back in his chair and looked directly at his young assistant, Officer Gilet.

'What do you mean by that, Inspector?' Gilet looked puzzled.

'My father always says that. "Everyone has his Vichy." Everyone has his version of what happened during the Occupation. Apparently our murder victim had his version, too. He was writing his memoirs.'

Corbet glanced around his office as though looking for something. He put his worn Livre de Poche copy of Stendhal's *Le Rouge et le noir* back on the shelf behind his desk. He would have to leave the hero, Julien Sorel, at the monastery in Besançon, in the company of his colleagues who had joined the clergy merely to eat well.

'They suspect poison,' Corbet said out of the corner of his mouth. 'He's called François de La Roche. Lives in the lst. Happened on the train coming from Bordeaux. They stopped at the hospital at Poitiers to have him looked at. He's on his way here in an ambulance. They suspect poison,' he repeated as he reached into his side drawer for a gold box engraved with the bold letters *Marquise de Sévigné* and popped one of his favourite chocolates into his mouth.

Inspector Corbet settled his solid body snugly into his chair like a great bear trying to get comfortable. The early morning sun piercing in from a window over his head highlighted his silver-streaked, ash-blond hair, giving it a divine glow. The large gallic nose in the ruggedly hand-some face spoke of his provincial heritage. He rested his round cinnamon-brown eyes on Gilet, who stretched to his full height, crossed his arms and stared back at him in silence. Gilet was a tall, slender man in his late thirties. Women had always found him irresistible, and he did not hesitate to use his charm when it might get him what he wanted.

'We'll soon find out for sure. You've called Ménager?' Gilet waited.

'But of course.' Corbet ate another chocolate. Gilet moved aside to let the powerful body of Officer Leroux pass through the door into Corbet's office. Leroux's bulk and dark, heavy features contrasted sharply with Gilet's light lankiness.

'Inspector, we've got another one. Last night, over on the rue du Mont Thabor. Took place in a restaurant, La Semaine.' Leroux was breathless.

'Who's the lucky person?' Years of dealing with death, deception and disappointment had fostered in Corbet a sense of hyperbole tinged with sarcasm and irony. He liked to think it had something to do with protecting his sanity.

'Roger Albert. Professor at the Sorbonne. They're look-ing for poison.'

'In that one too? I'm waiting for the body of de La Roche to arrive from Poitiers. I need to talk to his son and his wife. Leroux, you start with the Albert case. Talk to the people at the restaurant, his family and close acquaintances.'

'He was with a woman at the restaurant. I'll get her name and start with her.' Leroux's ruddy eagerness let Corbet know he was pleased to be included in the murder investigation of someone so important.

'Fine. I'm on my way to talk to the son of François de La Roche. Gilet, you go on down to Poitiers to talk to the local police, the people at the hospital, and those from the train who were held there.' Corbet felt like a general issuing orders to his soldiers before an important battle.

'Will do,' Gilet affirmed.

Corbet knew that his assistant loved to travel and would welcome the chance to get out of Paris for a little while. He leaned back in his chair, clasped his hands behind his golden head and heaved his great shoulders in a sigh.

Chapter Three

The bright afternoon sunshine bathed the little street in splendour as Inspector Corbet stood in front of the large oak door of the de La Roche residence at 37 rue du Mont Thabor. Just two doors down at 39 he noticed the discreet little sign, La Semaine. He pushed gently on the door of 37 that was half open at this hour of the day. As he stepped into the courtyard he came face-to-face with a slick-haired man with a sallow complexion. It was Pierre de La Roche.

'Inspector Corbet, Paris Police.'

'Yes, Inspector, I've been expecting you. Do come in.' Corbet followed Pierre into the corridor leading to the elevator.

In the close quarters of the small elevator, Corbet breathed in the fumes of garlic from Pierre's breath. He loved garlic but not the second time around. He began to wonder whether the aftermath of one of his escargot feasts had the same effect on those he encountered the next day.

The elevator crept slowly up the three flights. Pierre opened the door on to the landing and then turned left towards the great oak doors of the de La Roche apartment. It was luxurious indeed, full of what was probably Louis XV original furniture. There were precious tapestries on the walls, which looked like Gobelins. Corbet noticed that several large gilt mirrors gave the double sitting-rooms an added sense of space and drama. These were objects which had obviously been in the family for years.

Once inside and seated on a satin-upholstered sofa, Inspector Corbet began his inquiry.

'Sorry about your father.'

'Thank you.' Pierre spoke with the numb restraint and dignity of someone who has just lost a close loved one. He kept pushing back his already too slick, dark hair from the sides of his head, as through trying to soothe himself in the process.

'Had you noticed anything unusual about him in the past month or so? Did he seem to feel all right? Not sick or anything?' Corbet returned to the inquiry.

'He seemed fine. He was always a very busy man, never happy unless he was involved in some project. He had been working on a set of memoirs about his experiences in the Vichy government during the war. Spent most of his early mornings with his editor. I think the book was pretty close to completion, but I'm not sure. He never really shared much of that with me. He lost his first family in the war, and I was born a number of years after that. He never recovered from that loss.' Pierre seemed to need to talk.

At the mention of Vichy, Corbet again remembered that phrase he had so often heard his father utter, 'Everyone has his Vichy'. At that time many of his countrymen, motivated at best by survival, had collaborated with the German enemy in ridding the country of Jews. It was a reaction and a stance of which no one was very proud, and, so, it was often blanketed with a kind of blind denial, an amnesia. Corbet looked up at Pierre, who seemed to be waiting to go on.

'So, you weren't really close to him?' Corbet urged him to continue.

'Not really. He was polite but never really warm and loving. My mother made up for that, though,' he rushed to add. Corbet noticed small rings of dirt under Pierre's long fingernails. He fiddled with a copy of *La Noblesse* which lay on the coffee table.

'You know that my father wasn't the only aristocrat in our family. Mother comes from an even older line.' He cocked his head to one side as if to emphasise the point.

'No, I didn't,' Corbet responded dryly. 'She's not home yet?' he inquired.

'She'll be a bit delayed. They're involved in the grape harvest at the château, and she had to stay a little longer than she would have liked.'

Corbet frowned. Her husband had just died under suspicious circumstances, and she was tending to the grape harvest at the château!

'She was his second wife?' he inquired, even though he knew the answer.

'Yes. He married Mother some time after the war. She's thirty years younger than he. I guess you know that.' Corbet didn't but just nodded for him to continue.

'He was very lonely after he lost his family. In addition to being remarkably beautiful, Mother cheered him up. He needed that. It didn't work for long, however. He always seemed gloomy and preoccupied. Mother had to work hard not to be dragged down by his melancholy and brooding. That's where I came in.' Pierre shifted in his chair and smoothed his hair again, as though giving himself a gestural pat on the back.

'That's where you came in how?' Pierre was not appealing. There was something a little too sleek, too glib about him. Unctuous was the word.

'Yes, Mother and I were really more like best friends than mother and son. We did so much together.' As he relaxed, Pierre began to pass from a smooth, subtle delivery to one more marked with a slightly feminine gesture and tone of voice. His neck became loose, and his head went very easily from side to side. He turned his hands in an emphatic way. This change intrigued Corbet. He was trying not to notice a sour smell that seemed to fill the apartment. It wasn't exactly body odour but a musty, unclean smell, easily as offensive as the garlic he had smelled in the elevator. He decided that this was the time to get to a very important point.

'Your father died at about 8 p.m. last night. Where were you when this happened?'

'Oh, I was here at the apartment. Mother left me in charge of welcoming an American student who will be living in our studio next door for the academic term. She feels that she's making some sort of contribution to better world understanding by renting the studio to foreign students.'

Corbet wondered whether having a lodger didn't also help with the frightful cost of living in Paris.

'The young woman arrived here last night, and I helped her settle in. A rather nice young lady but a bit like a frightened rabbit. The journey here seemed to have taken its toll on her.'

'Where did she come from?' Corbet expected to hear New York, Boston, Chicago.

'Oh, she came in on the train from Bordeaux last night. She was there visiting friends. I had hoped Mother would be able to interview her, but she was too busy with the problems at the château. She said she felt she could rely on my judgement, as usual.'

Pierre smiled an oily smile, took a deep breath and continued. 'In fact, it might have been the same train that my father was on. I got the call about his death while she was here in the apartment, but they didn't tell me at first that he had died on a train. I didn't know he was coming up from Bordeaux last night. It must have been a last-minute decision.'

He brushed the left side of his head, once again smoothing his already glued-back hair. 'He may not even have notified Mother. Often he didn't. Just left when he felt like it, especially lately.'

'Well, have you talked with the young woman since last night?' Corbet wanted to be sure to track down this little detail.

'I knocked, but she hasn't been in. I'll speak to her later.'

'I'd rather you didn't. Why don't you wait and let me talk to her first.' He wanted to begin at the beginning with her.

'Fine. If that's the way you want to do it. I don't really…' The jangling of the phone stopped Pierre in mid-sentence, and he reached for the receiver.

'*Allô.* Why, of course, Mother. I understand.' He held the phone in his right hand and began to shuffle through some papers on the desk holding the phone. He seemed to be looking for something.

'A very severe storm, you say. Were all of the vineyards affected?' There was a pause in which Madame de La Roche gave a long accounting.

'Well, at least you've salvaged that. No, I'm sure he'll understand. I'll tell them. Please don't concern yourself with it.' Pierre seemed to have found what he was looking for on the desk.

'Yes, I will, and, of course, I do.' His tone became light and even a bit flirtatious.

'*A bientôt.*' He hung up and turned to Corbet. 'Sorry, Inspector, but my mother informs me that she'll have to remain in Bordeaux for at least another couple of days. They've had some very severe storms that have almost wiped out the harvest. She must oversee the clean-up and salvage of the vines. Jules Flagon, the head estate worker, has suddenly taken off for parts unknown and Mother has been left very short-handed. I would go down myself, but we feel some member of the family has to stay here in Paris while the investigation goes on, and see to Father's body.' He flung his hand at Corbet as though for emphasis.

Corbet gazed at him in dismay. 'Well, what's the address and telephone number of the château? I'll have to go down there to talk to her.'

'But, really, she'll be very, very preoccupied,' Pierre insisted as he wrote the address and telephone number on a piece of paper he had gotten from the desk.

'But of course,' clipped Corbet. 'Of course she will.' He rose to take the paper from Pierre's hand.

'By the way, there was a murder last night next door in the restaurant, La Semaine. What do you know about that?' Corbet waited.

'Well, Inspector, I read about that in the paper today, but last night I heard nothing. After I left Rachel Todd, I went right to bed. My room is way in the back of the apartment, and once I'm back there, I never hear anything that goes on in the street.' Pierre smoothed his hair again.

'Very well.' Corbet headed toward the door. 'I'll talk to you later.' He closed the door behind him and pressed for the small elevator. The slight odour of garlic reminded him that he was hungry. With all of this, he had missed lunch.

Chapter Four

'Inspector Corbet, Paris Police. I'm here to check the crime scene.' La Semaine had closed its doors to customers. Corbet was led into the little room he had often occupied when dining there. The decor of pink and white linen and the Louis XV reproduction furniture gave a sense of elegance he normally found in much larger restaurants. His stomach growled, and he wished he could sit down and order his favourite white asparagus soufflé. Henri Oliver, the owner of the restaurant, approached.

'They've got us all roped off, Inspector. Horrible thing that happened. My staff is very upset.'

'Well, I'm afraid you'll have to remain closed at least for the rest of the day, Henri. Sorry. There's not much I can do about it.' Corbet noticed that a table in the corner was cordoned off with yellow tape.

'Any eyewitnesses to what happened?' Corbet waited.

'Well, he was with a woman. They were the only ones in the restaurant, other than the serving staff.' Henri seemed agitated.

'When Albert actually died, did anyone see it?'

Corbet could smell the stale cooking odours from last night's offerings.

'Only the woman he was with. They were having dessert. My staff was in the back beginning to clean up. It was late. They were our last customers.'

'Thank you very much, Henri. Sorry for the inconvenience. My men will go over the scene one more time, and then you can open up again. Good luck.' Corbet headed out on to the rue du Mont Thabor. He would take the Métro.

As he turned down the rue de Castiglione, he passed one of his favourite antique bookstores. They had a wonderful selection of books from old estates at pretty good prices. Just last month he had purchased a red leather-bound, four-volume edition of Balzac's letters to his mistress, Madame Hanska. Poor Balzac had spent many years writing to a married woman who lived in Poland. He was finally able to marry her some years after her husband died. Unfortunately, shortly after the marriage, Balzac's heart gave out, and he died. Corbet had always found this irony particularly poignant. He was convinced that if he ever were able to connect with the love of his life, he might well be deprived of enjoying it.

He thought back to his days at the Sorbonne when he had met a woman who might have been the love of his life. She had married an Italian aristocrat and, as far as he knew, was still living in Venice. While he loved Italy, he never had been able to visit Venice.

The bookstore was closed, and he eyed its window displays with regret, wishing he could spend some time browsing. He reluctantly left the windows and headed for the rue de Rivoli, turning left down towards the Tuileries Métro stop. The elaborate preparations for the bicentennial celebration of the Revolution were underway across the street in the Tuileries. Corbet found it hard to believe that in less than a year, in July of 1989, the great festivities would occupy all of Paris. As he neared the place where he would cross the street to the Métro stop, the window of the Angelina tea room beckoned. He entered, took in its faded gentility and remembered that at the beginning of the century, when it was known as Rumpelmayer's, it was frequented by none other than Marcel Proust.

The waitress brought his order of crème de marron Chantilly, and he attacked with relish the taupe-coloured mound of puréed chestnut topped with sinful whipped cream. It soothed his hunger. He would have to phone Gilet and let him know he was going to stop in Poitiers on the way to Bordeaux. Gilet had a lot of potential, and Corbet liked him. Maybe he was just a little too eager.

A couple of tables over he noticed a young couple leaning towards each other in intense conversation. He couldn't hear what they were saying. The young man took her hand and held it. Corbet kept looking at them, knowing that they were too absorbed in each other to notice him. Years ago that could have been he and his love. The script could have turned out differently. It always could in love. It always could, even in murder. It was too bad one couldn't interview the victim in a murder case. What would François de La Roche have said for himself?

Corbet realised there was no point in straining to overhear the conversation. He couldn't but was sure that it was about matters much more pleasant that those that confronted him. The mound of crème de marron Chantilly had disappeared, having provided its temporary refuge. He paid the bill, left Angelina and headed for his apartment to pack for his stay in Bordeaux.

Chapter Five

Inspector Henri Corbet lived in the 6th arrondissement at 13 rue de Buci, near the Odéon stop on the Métro. He loved his quartier because there were many outdoor markets where he could buy the best of fruits, meats and vegetables to indulge his passion for cooking.

The second-hand and foreign bookstores catered to his love of history and literature. He knew most about French history but had more than a nodding acquaintance with the histories of both Russia and Germany. Uncovering people's motives and looking at the worst side of human nature could be depressing without the soothing comfort of food well-prepared and a sense of history that told him that man has always been a rather mixed lot and that crime and criminals haven't essentially changed but have merely taken different forms.

He climbed the stairs to his four-room apartment and opened the door on to a sitting-room whose focal point was a carved, white marble fireplace. The antique sofas, covered in black leather and facing one another, looked inviting after a day at work. Corbet glanced expectantly around the room as though looking for someone.

'Michelet? Michelet?' No one replied. 'Oh, now, where have you been hiding yourself? Come out and welcome me home.' A large black and white cat strolled out of an adjoining room, blinking the sleep out of his eyes. He greeted Corbet with a rather subtle 'meow' for a cat his size. When he reached Corbet's legs, he began to circle them and purr. Corbet picked him up, gave him a hug, then put him down and headed for the kitchen.

He washed his hands well and then opened the door to a small refrigerator and took out a package of the pastry dough he had been letting rest. It was his firm belief that his own croissants were the best, and, so, he took the time when he could to make the light and flaky crescent-shaped pastry from many, many layers of butter and flour.

He laid the dough down on the counter and reached for his large pastry rolling-pin to give it another turn. Surrounded by his copper cooking pots from Dehillerin, as well as all sorts of kitchen gadgets used in his hobby, he was king of his realm as he gently poked his creation to see if it had rested long enough.

As he rolled the dough, he began to consider the case at hand. He had sent Gilet down to Poitiers to interview people and talk to those at the hospital where the dead man had been taken when he was removed from the train. He would talk to him on his way to Bordeaux. Ménager was working on the body now.

How odd, he thought, as I am here rolling out dough, Ménager is cutting open the body of a dead man to find out how he died. As he gave the dough another turn, he was glad that he was working on flour and butter and not on human flesh.

The dead man, François de La Roche, lived on the rue du Mt. Thabor in the lst in pretty fancy living quarters. He was obviously one of those Frenchmen who still clung to his noble heritage, as the *particule* in front of his name attested. Really, some of them didn't seem to realise there had been a Revolution. Corbet finished the turn of his pastry and returned it to the refrigerator for another rest.

He began to think about his interview with Pierre. Naturally, one had to suspect the persons closest if it were not an accidental death. He wondered what kind of hidden layers of twisted human emotion lay behind those relationships. What would he find in Bordeaux with Thérèse de La Roche? He washed off his rolling-pin.

The ring of the phone jostled him out of his reverie.

'*Allô*,' he said, holding the phone in the space between his chin and shoulder while he dried his hands. 'Oh, Gilet, yes. I was about to call you. What have you come up with?' He listened to the voice on the other end of the phone.

'They say it was definitely poison, and Ménager and the toxicologist are running tests for the various categories. They won't know exactly what it was until tomorrow, but it looks like cyanide. We're trying to trace the people who were seated around him on the train.'

'When do you think you'll get back to Paris?'

'Probably by tomorrow. I only have a few more people to talk to here. Are you going to talk to the son yourself?'

'I already have. I'll be coming down to Bordeaux tomorrow to talk to the wife. Says she can't leave because of the grape harvests. I don't want to lose any time, so, I'm leaving tomorrow morning. You stay there. I'll call you when I get into Poitiers.'

'Sure thing.' Gilet seemed glad to be ordered to stay away from Paris a little longer.

Corbet hung up the receiver and stared into space, wondering what he would find at the end of his investigation. The phone rang again.

'Yes,' he answered. It was Leroux. 'What have you found out?'

'I've talked to the woman who was with Albert in the restaurant when he died. She's pretty distraught, but I was able to get some information. He was a professor at the Sorbonne. A big shot there, working on some book on Proust.'

'Have they verified the cause of death yet?'

'No, not yet. They suspect poison but aren't sure. Ménager is working on another case right now and won't be available to start the investigation until tomorrow.'

'The François de La Roche case?' inquired Corbet.

'Yes,' said Leroux.

'Very interesting. Have you begun to question his close associates?'

'I've only talked to the woman who was with him at the restaurant. Marie Marceau, his girlfriend for some time. She's really broken up. Says that he hadn't really been himself for some time. She thought it was because of the pressure of his work, but now she isn't sure. Says she can't imagine who would want to kill him.'

'What did you say her name was?' Corbet couldn't disguise his impatience.

'Marie Marceau,' Leroux replied.

'I'll take over with her. I want to talk to her later,' Corbet interjected, cutting off the flow of information. He wanted to start from scratch with this woman, if possible, especially if she turned out to be who he thought she was.

He hung up the receiver. It's probably not the same woman, and there may be no connection between the cases, he reassured himself somewhat feebly, but it does look like the same method of operation.

Chapter Six

The train from Paris approached Poitiers. Corbet tucked his paperback copy of Zola's *Thérèse Raquin* in his briefcase. He shuddered as he did so at the thought of the violent and tragic consequences of the love triangle in the book. The graphic description of the corpse of the murdered husband in the morgue was haunting, and the power of guilt to mete out its own punishment fascinating.

Gilet would be waiting for him at the station. He had telephoned ahead to Madame de La Roche to indicate that he would be coming down to talk to her. She had consented to meet with him but had indicated that she was very preoccupied with her vineyards. Her deep, throaty voice had been a bit of a surprise. He wasn't really sure what he had expected, but somehow it wasn't that voice.

She had suggested that he come for dinner since they were out in the country where it would be difficult for him to find a place to eat at the hour he would be arriving, and why didn't he stay the night? There was plenty of guest space. At the château they ate a late dinner, starting around 9 p.m. That time would suit him fine.

He felt a bit uneasy at the prospect of dining with someone whom he was questioning about a murder, especially one that might have involved poison. In any event, it was not standard procedure. But then not much about this family and this case seemed very ordinary.

As he descended from the train he saw Gilet's long form running to meet him. Everything about him spoke of extension and speed.

'I'm sure glad you're here.' Gilet plunged right in without catching his breath. 'I've not come up with very much, but I'll tell you what I have.'

At this point, he drew a deep breath and began. 'The people who were near him on the train were made to get off and stay here for questioning.'

'Go on,' Corbet nodded.

'A woman who was sitting across from him said she had noticed that since boarding the train at Bordeaux de La Roche had been very absorbed in reading what looked like a manuscript. In fact, it was his book, his memoirs. He was reading a draft of that. When the vendor came around to sell snacks, de La Roche bought a drink and then began to eat some sort of cake that he took out of a white linen napkin. That's all she noticed until he ran into difficulty breathing and seemed to choke. By then the woman was so distressed that she doesn't remember much after that, except for a blur of people around tending to the man.'

'A man who was sitting in front of him said he had noticed a rather distracted looking man in his late thirties or early forties. He said that he had come up and down the aisle several times just before de La Roche got into trouble. We were unable to locate anyone fitting that description out of the people we were able to detain.'

'The manuscript, napkin and teacup have, of course, been saved?' Corbet inquired, looking at Gilet with an abstracted air.

'Oh, yes, we have those, along with a monogrammed silver pillbox which contained artificial sweetener tablets laced with cyanide. Not too difficult to determine that that's what killed him.'

'What about the napkin?' Corbet pressed.

'Funny thing about that,' Gilet hastened to add. 'There was a monogrammed symbol on the napkin, like a family crest, a lion's head between two crossed swords, I think. It was also on the pillbox.'

'Interesting,' Corbet mused. 'I understand de La Roche was from the noblesse and that he had a very royalist bent. Where did he get the napkin?'

'Apparently brought it with him. Had some cakes wrapped in it. The crumbs tested indicate they were madeleines.'

'Madeleines? Very strange. Indeed, very strange.' Corbet often enjoyed the little lemon-flavoured cakes as a snack at night.

'I'm on my way down to Bordeaux to talk to Madame de La Roche. She won't be back in Paris for a few days, and I can't wait. Leroux has begun the Albert investigation.'

'Oh, the one who died in the restaurant near the de La Roche apartment?' Corbet nodded. He began again to wonder whether there was more than a coincidence of propinquity connecting these two deaths.

Chapter Seven

After re-boarding the train to continue his journey, Corbet sat quietly musing over what he had learned from Gilet and wondering what he would encounter at Château de La Roche-Carnet. He decided not to continue with his reading of Zola but to doze a bit. He might very well have a late night. Arriving at the Bordeaux train station at nightfall, he got a taxi and headed for the château.

'What do you know about the de La Roche family?' he inquired of the taxi-driver.

'Château de La Roche-Carnet, a beautiful old country house with very productive vineyards. The wine is one of the more famous in the area. Next to Margaux or Pomerol, it's one of the best.'

'I mean the family, the people,' insisted Corbet.

'Well, Madame de La Roche is – how shall I say it? She's very, very beautiful, very appealing to a man, if you know what I mean.'

Corbet didn't exactly. He pressed, 'What do you mean, *appealing*?'

'Well, she speaks to men. She has a figure you notice and don't forget. She almost hypnotises you with her voice.'

'Yes, that voice,' mused Corbet. 'How do you know so much about her?'

'Well, at times she uses the taxi service to come to the train station. I sometimes see her then. Other times she has her own driver, Jules Flagon. I know him. He works on her estate. He goes to one of the local cafés where I go. He talks a lot about her. That's mostly how I know. I've seen her a few times though. Flagon is quite mad about her.'

'Quite mad about her?' Corbet probed. 'He's married?'

'But of course. He just appreciates Madame de La Roche.'

'You don't think there's something between them, do you?' Corbet continued to press.

'Oh, no, only in Jules's mind,' he stated with assurance.

The taxi was now winding down rather narrow roads flanked on either side by lines of the most carefully groomed vineyards Corbet had ever seen. Even in the dusk it was a magnificent sight. The manicured order of the vines along the road was somehow reassuring. After a bit, the driver turned right into a driveway bordered on each side with rows and rows of neat vines. At the end of the very long driveway the cab drove in a circle up to the heavy, wooden door of the château. Corbet paid the driver, thanked him, got out of the cab and headed for the brass knocker.

'Come in, Monsieur l'Inspecteur.' The butler showed him into the great hall. Standing in awe on the black and white tiles, Corbet removed his coat and waited for Madame de La Roche.

At the end of the hallway there was a large and very long staircase. Corbet's eye followed to the top of it where the most beautiful woman he had ever seen stood. Her honey-coloured hair was swept back and up on her head, and she was clothed in a long green velveteen dress which showed off her lovely, bare shoulders and outlined her ample but perfectly formed breasts. Even at that distance there was something that radiated from her. Corbet clutched his hands and waited for her to descend. She did so one careful step at a time, her movements subtly serpentine but not openly seductive. Corbet stood mesmerised.

'We'll go into the library for an apéritif first.' Her soft, throaty voice and the gesture of her long, slender arm lured Corbet into the library at the right of the entrance hall.

His eyes took in the rows and rows of leather-bound volumes, books that must have been in the de La Roche family for many years. He checked his urge to begin an eager examination of the titles. Thérèse de La Roche poured out some port from a large decanter and handed a glass to Corbet. He took it greedily, glad to have something to clutch in his hand, something that might quiet the agitation that being in the presence of Thérèse de La Roche was generating. He would worry about what might be in the glass later.

'Did you have a smooth journey down from Paris?' she inquired. Apparently she had decided to take the lead by asking the questions. Corbet could do nothing for the moment but let her.

'Yes, quite pleasant and uneventful. Rather unlike that of your husband's from Bordeaux to Paris.' He recovered his composure enough to remember why he had come down to the château. Thérèse de La Roche glanced at him with lowered eyelids masking an expression it was hard to read.

'Ah, yes, François, we will miss him terribly. Awful business this is.' She clutched her glass tightly.

'Poisoned with cyanide, cyanide in his tea.' Corbet seemed to be trying to imprint the ugly circumstances on her mind as well as his own.

'Can you think of anyone who would want him dead?' He was trying hard to stay on course.

'Well, I've been wondering that since I got the news. You know that he had held many important positions in the government?'

'Yes,' Corbet affirmed, boldly swallowing his drink and again glancing at the rows of leather-bound volumes. 'A manuscript was found near the body, memoirs of his government service and experiences during the Second World War.'

'Yes, he had been working very hard on that for some time. He was almost finished with it. His editor was like his shadow, always visiting, calling, coming to our Paris apartment or down here to talk to François about something or other to do with the manuscript. He kept wanting him to make changes, to delete certain things. François was not very happy about that. He really didn't want to censor his work. The editor, of course, wanted to get it published and not disturb any of those in high positions with unsettling revelations. François wanted to tell the truth. They were always quarrelling. In fact, François was considering just finishing the manuscript and letting it be published posthumously.' Once she started, Thérèse, like Pierre, seemed to seize the opportunity to unburden herself to Inspector Corbet.

Corbet watched her closely as she related her story. That she was magically beautiful was an understatement.

By Corbet's calculation she was a woman of at least fifty, but she had the kind of beauty with which only a few women were blessed, one that would probably hold well into old age. The secret seemed to be in the bone structure of the face.

'Had he made a final decision in that regard?' Corbet resumed the interrogation.

'Not yet. I think he was going to make that decision, though.'

'Do you know if his editor had any idea of his possible change in plans? And, by the way, what house was he with?'

'Galliante. Monsieur Simon. No. He had only discussed it with me and a few close friends. If he knew of it, it wasn't from François.'

'It's possible that someone got to Monsieur Simon with the rumour, then?' Corbet closed in.

'I suppose it could have happened.' Thérèse said very softy, as though considering this possibility for the first time.

'Dinner is served, Madame.' The butler's announcement came from the library door.

Thérèse put down her glass and with a sweep of her long arm again indicated that they should proceed through the door and into the dining-room.

Corbet was dazzled by the table set with a full service of nineteenth-century Sèvres, Odiot silver and Lalique crystal, evidently heirlooms, underlined by the splendour of a white damask tablecloth. The butler ushered Thérèse to her seat at the head of the table and motioned for Corbet to sit on her right-hand side so that they might avoid talking across a long table.

Once again Corbet struggled to regain his composure and gather strength to finish his inquiry. The butler brought a lovely steaming tureen of consommé. The smell was intoxicating as Corbet let him fill his soup bowl with the delectable liquid. Garnishing the consommé with the julienne of vegetables provided him by the butler, he took up the sword again.

'So, if Simon had found out about this possibility, he would not have liked it, we can assume?'

'Probably not,' agreed Thérèse. 'But I don't know how he could have found out.'

'Who were your husband's closest friends?' Corbet punctuated the inquiry with a delicious spoonful of consommé.

'He had some friends who were with him in the government during the war, but most of them have died now. There was one relatively new friend, Roger Albert. He had met him through his editor. The man is also a writer, a professor of literature at the Sorbonne. François was very private about many things.'

'What about relatives?' Corbet continued. She obviously didn't know yet about Albert's fate, or if she did, she wasn't letting on.

'Well, François had outlived his brother and sister. There are probably some cousins, but we didn't keep in touch with them.'

'What about his first family? Anyone at all left from that?'

'Only Valérie Ribeau. She's his first wife's sister. She and François were never close, but since the death of Hélène there had been much more distance between them. He always felt that Valérie blamed him for Hélène's death. They were part Jewish, you know, and when the Germans found out, François's position was no protection against Hélène's being deported to Poland into a camp.'

'Valérie was hidden by her adopted family. The only contact we've maintained with her is to rent our former maid's quarters as a studio apartment for foreign students during their stay in Paris. Valérie is much too practical to ignore the housing shortage and makes use of the connection. She works for Bryn Mawr College's study abroad program.' Thérèse seemed to need to continue, but Corbet interrupted her.

'So, you rent to a student? Who's there now?'

'An American woman. Rachel Todd, I think her name is. I haven't met her. Pierre has settled her in. As a matter of fact, she arrived on the night François was killed. I think Valérie said she was coming up on the train from Bordeaux.'

'Do you think she came on the same train as Monsieur de La Roche?' Corbet took another spoonful of the consommé.

'It could very well be. Pierre would know when she arrived. You should ask him.'

'I've done that. He doesn't know,' Corbet replied.

'Was he a difficult man to live with?' He returned to the subject of François.

'Not at first. But after a short while a melancholy seemed to descend, to cover his whole life. He was sombre and very serious most of the time. There was something that seemed to be consuming him. He would never let me close enough to discuss it, if he even knew what it was.'

Thérèse spoke very slowly and deliberately, as though deep in thought about what she was saying. Her consommé was cooling without much attention from her. Corbet, on the other hand, was managing nicely to consume his and was struggling not to let his gaze fall on her for too long lest he not be able to retrieve it.

The butler cleared the soup plates and brought another plate of sautéed, fresh goose liver with raisins, a speciality of the region. Corbet could barely contain his delight at the prospect of eating such a delicacy prepared by someone who, the consommé had testified, knew his business. He helped himself gladly from the plate held out by the butler, as did Madame de La Roche. She motioned for the butler to fill the wine glasses, which he did from a bottle bearing the Château de La Roche-Carnet label.

Corbet's enthusiasm made him unable to wait the polite time for Thérèse to take the first bite. He cut the delicacy and put the first morsel into his mouth before she had even picked up her fork. The perfection of the burst of flavours was a joy. He wondered how he could get the recipe from the cook and began to speculate on how he might duplicate it himself. Obviously, the goose liver had been sautéed with onions and carrots for flavour and then a demi-glace was made and laced with cognac. Yes, that might work. Once the sauce was reduced, the raisins could be added and simmered in. He would experiment with this at home.

'We have several more courses,' warned Thérèse as she watched the relish with which Corbet consumed his goose liver. She began to pick at hers.

'Oh, yes, excuse me.' He became somewhat self-conscious. 'But it's so very good. I don't suppose you would give me the recipe?'

'Jean never parts with his secrets.' Thérèse ended the pursuit.

Slightly disappointed and remembering the purpose of his visit, Corbet continued the inquiry. 'So, François never told you what was disturbing him? Never hinted at what it might be?' He took a long drink of the dark red wine. It was deep and mellow.

'Not really. He had never gotten over losing his family in the war. At first I thought I was going to make a difference in his life. He seemed to perk up after he met me, but that didn't last. He was very withdrawn and spent a lot of time reading and writing. He seemed to prefer solitude.'

The butler cleared the goose liver course. Corbet watched him remove Thérèse's half-full plate and wished he dared to volunteer to finish the uneaten portions. He checked himself. The next course was roast venison with a red Bordeaux sauce with shallots. He helped himself from the platter held out by the butler and immediately regretted his prior gluttony with the goose liver. He hoped he would have enough room to enjoy the venison. This time he could wait for Thérèse to begin eating hers.

'It must have been lonely for you?' he probed.

He took another deep drink of the luscious wine.

'Yes, but I had my son, Pierre, and that made a lot of difference to me. François never seemed to show much interest in him, seemed to look through him. I tried to make up for this, but I don't know how well I've done.' She seemed to be drifting off again. The butler brought a platter of deep green asparagus bathed in lemon butter.

'The night your husband left Bordeaux to take the train to Paris, did you notice anything unusual about him?' Corbet got back on track.

'Not really. He was going up to Paris to meet with his editor. I was going to follow a few days later. This was before we had the storm down here and I had to stay. My head estate worker had a family emergency and wasn't available to help me with things here, and with the grape harvests and the storm destroying a lot of the vines, I couldn't leave.' Thérèse seemed to have lost sight of the original question about François's state of mind and was more interested in explaining her own.

The roast venison was delightful. It was done perfectly, and the wine sauce was rich and vibrant. Thérèse seemed slow to appreciate hers. She obviously didn't share his passion for food.

'There was a monogrammed napkin and a monogrammed silver pillbox found near the body. The pillbox contained artificial sweetener laced with cyanide, the poison that killed him. The napkin had a monogram of a family crest, a lion's head between two crossed swords, and there were crumbs that were identified as madeleine crumbs. What do you know about that?'

'Well, the napkin comes from our linen supply. The monogram is the de La Roche coat of arms. Jean probably sent François off with a supply of madeleines for the train ride. The silver pillbox was a gift from Pierre. François used artificial sweetener because he was hypoglycaemic.'

'He didn't by any chance bring the tea with him?'

'I doubt it.' She pushed her plate away from her.

The butler, taking the cue, came to remove the dinner plates. Corbet had managed to finish his venison and was feeling pleasantly satisfied by the wondrous food and the splendid wine. His sense of well-being was short-lived as he remembered that he was approaching the most delicate part of the interrogation and would have to do that through the cheese course.

A large tray of fruit and cheese was set before him. He viewed it with some interest and waited politely until Thérèse had taken the first pieces.

'The night Monsieur de La Roche took the train from Bordeaux to Paris, you were here at the château?' he began with temerity.

'Oh, yes. I was going to stay down for a couple more days until the harvest was under control. François didn't like to occupy himself too much with the details of running the vineyards. He preferred to leave that to me and Jules.'

'Who took him to the station?' Corbet pressed further.

'Why, probably Jules. Actually, I don't remember. If Jules didn't, it was probably the local cab company.'

'This Jules, he's your head hired worker?' The roquefort was mellow and rich, but Corbet was already very full.

'Yes. I don't know what I'd do without him. His family has been with the vineyards for generations. He knows how to grow grapes and all about running a vineyard.' Thérèse spoke with some enthusiasm.

'How old a man is he?' Corbet remembered what the cab driver had told him on his way to the château.

'Oh, he's probably in his late thirties,' Thérèse said readily.

'Now, Madame de La Roche, can you remember exactly what you might have been doing at the time your husband died, which would have been about 8 p.m. Saturday evening?' He had to close in. He drained his wine glass.

'Well, let me see. I was probably in my room reading. I have an early dinner when I'm dining alone and often retire to my room to read. I have to get up early to oversee the running of the vineyards. So, yes, I believe I was just finishing Stendhal's *Le Rouge et le noir*. It's one of my favourites. I can't seem to read it too many times.'

Corbet registered this information with some interest. It was the same book about attempted murder and execution that he had been reading. The hero Julien Sorel's acts of violence were certainly romanticised and his brutal ambition somehow justified on its own grounds by the author. Or so some of the critics said. Corbet couldn't help sharing Stendhal's partiality to his hero.

'Well, that's chilling bedtime reading.'

'However misguided, they are people who go after what they want. That intrigues me.' She seemed almost wistful.

'Now, I'm afraid I have to ask you some very personal questions,' Corbet tried to enter gently.

'Before you do, let's retire to the drawing-room.' Thérèse rose and led the way. As the butler prepared to serve the coffee and Armagnac, she looked steadily at Corbet.

'Yes, Inspector?' she said expectantly, seating herself in a large throne chair by the fireplace.

'Your relationship with your husband, would you say it was a happy one?' He decided on a long approach. He seated himself in the matching throne chair.

'Well, that's hard to say. We didn't quarrel, if that's what you mean. Were we close? Did we communicate a lot? No. But I think you mean something other than that?'

'I do,' admitted Corbet. 'Did you have a lover?' He got to the point with a deep drink of his coffee.

'I – well, yes. Yes, I have had lovers.'

'What can you tell me about him or them?' Corbet waited.

'Well, there really hasn't been one long-standing person. Living with François hasn't been easy. He was remote. We have not shared the same bed for years. That was over very soon after our marriage. I have amused myself as I can. I decided that I didn't want to fall in love with anyone. It would make things too complicated. This way it's better.

Nobody gets hurt.' She stared into the fireplace as if there were some answer in the flames.

'Did Monsieur de La Roche know about your liaisons?' Corbet was going in for the finish.

'I suppose he suspected. I tried to be discreet, you know, but I'm sure he suspected. Never said anything though. It was just quietly understood between us,' she said softly, almost with reverence.

'Do you think that any of the men with whom you have been involved would have had any reason to want Monsieur de La Roche dead?'

'My God, no.' Thérèse laughed. 'No, not at all. I told you nobody ever got serious.' She became firm.

'Are you sure of that?' Corbet had a hard time believing that, imagining how he would react if she decided to bless him with her favours. He would be serious.

'I'm sure.' Thérèse smiled softly at him.

'Well, I don't mean to pry, but I will have to ask you to provide me with their names.' Corbet took a large swig of Armagnac.

'Why, Inspector Corbet, I don't really think it's any of your business.' Thérèse suddenly became very cold.

'In a murder investigation, Madame de La Roche, everything is my business.' Corbet eyed her steadily while she stared again into the fire. He must have waited for at least two minutes before she said something.

'There's no one right now, so what difference does it make if there were others in the past?' She looked at him with a rather blank expression.

'Anything to do with a marriage where one party has been murdered, past, present or otherwise, is significant.' Corbet would not be daunted.

'Sorry, Inspector, but I just don't feel comfortable revealing the names of these people to you.' She stood her ground.

'All right, Madame de La Roche. I'm sure that if it's relevant it will come out as I peel back the layers in this investigation. For the moment, I'll respect your privacy.'

With the most difficult part of the interrogation behind him, Corbet settled back in his chair and resolved to savour his coffee and Armagnac.

Chapter Eight

The next morning Corbet awoke from a sound sleep induced by his full stomach and the extra glass of Armagnac he had taken just before retiring.

Like Scarlet O'Hara, he had resolved to think of the troubling case at hand tomorrow. Tomorrow was here. He stretched his solid, round arms and legs and still felt a bit lost in the long Louis XV half-bed in which he had spent the night. It was a remarkable bed with a silk tapestry curtain and canopy covering it, creating a world of its own. It was the kind of place in which one could rest comfortably for the whole day with a good book.

Corbet considered how wonderful it would be if he were truly a guest at the château and could spend his evenings dining with and talking to Thérèse de La Roche and his days lounging in the library with the leather-bound volumes, taking now and again to the Louis XV bed for a nap and a read. It had been a long time since he had had the kind of vacation he adored, a reading, dining and resting one.

Something in the back of his mind wouldn't let him carry his fantasy too far, and he put his feet on the floor, knowing that he had to get on with the business at hand, which was to get back to Paris as soon as possible to talk with more people about these disturbing deaths. In addition to Marie Marceau, he wanted to talk to Valérie Ribeau and also to Rachel Todd, the student who rented the de La

Roche studio. He would try to get an appointment with Simon from Galliante.

The butler knocked and brought in a tray of hot coffee, croissants and fresh orange juice. Corbet bit into the buttery crescent. It was actually almost as good as his own. Not quite, but close. The fellow in the kitchen sure knew his business. He regretted that he would not have the opportunity to talk with him about the goose liver and the venison.

Dressed, bathed and fortified by his breakfast, he went by cab back to the station. Once on the train, he sat down and tried to imagine what it must have been like to have been François de La Roche heading for Paris with his manuscript in hand. Corbet had purchased a local Bordeaux paper at the train station and began to read it somewhat absently, pretending it was a creation of his own.

His attention was grabbed by a story on the second page. NEW SUSPECT SOUGHT IN UNSOLVED MURDER. He began to read with some interest. It seemed that about five years ago a local girl had been murdered. She had been pregnant, and somebody had brutally assaulted her with a knife. The identity of the murderer remained unknown. Her boyfriend at the time, the main suspect, had been acquitted at the trial. They didn't say who the new suspect was but hinted that it was someone whose family had been in the area for generations.

It happens everywhere, Corbet mused. Paris, Bordeaux, Provence. Everywhere. People killing other people for all kinds of sordid reasons. Maybe they would never find the killer. Indeed, maybe he would never solve the murders he was investigating. He began to feel somewhat despondent. The haunting memory of Thérèse de La Roche didn't help. He had fought valiantly not to come totally under her spell, but he had to admit that he was more drawn in than he liked. How could she have killed her husband? Perhaps she had had someone else do it? And then who would that be? He would just have to keep digging. He secretly hoped he would not find evidence that would lead to her guilt. Maybe it had to do with one of these other people. The editor, perhaps, or this Valérie Ribeau or even the American student. There must be something that he could learn from them that would lead him to the killer.

The thought of the other death began to intrude on him. He knew he had to go to the end to find out if there was a connection between them.

Chapter Nine

At the Gare d'Austerlitz he telephoned Gilet, who had returned earlier that morning, and made an appointment to meet him for lunch at Le Blason on the rue Saint Honoré in the lst. While taking the Métro to the Tuileries stop, Corbet tried to summarise what he had gotten from his interview with Madame de La Roche. Gilet would want to know all. However, there was no way he could really tell all. He hoped that the cold, penetrating eye of his assistant wouldn't discern his vulnerability to that haunting woman.

'*Bonjour*, Jacques.' He greeted the proprietor, a man from Provence who had come to Paris to make his fortune with a little brasserie. He had hardly done that but had managed to do quite a good business due to his location and the quality of his food.

'Omelette Parmentier?' Jacques inquired as he led Corbet to a table in the back.

'But of course.' When he came for lunch, he always had his favourite large omelette filled with sautéed potatoes and onions.

Just as he was seated, he looked up to see Gilet headed for him. With his long, determined stride he looked like a man with a mission.

'Good day, Inspector,' he began. 'Did you have a good trip down and back?'

'Very good. Very good train ride,' Corbet volunteered.

'Well, what happened? What did you find out?' Gilet was not going to stand on any kind of ceremony.

'No, first you tell me what you've been up to.' Corbet used his higher position to make this request which would give him more time.

Gilet was eager to begin the exchange no matter who went first. 'Yes, very well. This morning I talked to Marie Marceau, Albert's girlfriend. It's difficult to get anything out of her. She's in such a state of shock. I don't believe I've ever seen anyone so broken up about the death of a loved one. She says it's worse because they were somewhat estranged when he died. The poor woman is really suffering. I think maybe you'd better talk to her. You may have better luck than I did, and, also, more time has gone by.'

'Very well.' Corbet decided that he would not let Gilet know that he was really annoyed with his impetuous examination of Marie Marceau. He knew now that he really had to talk to her, and soon.

'Did you get anything on her background? Find out how long she has been connected with the Sorbonne?'

'Well, she did say that she had been in the academic world all her life. She did her studies at Paris III. Literature, I think it was. Taught for a bit and then married some Italian aristocrat and moved to Venice. She left there about fifteen years ago, returned to Paris and got divorced.'

'Her boyfriend, Albert, was a leading expert on Proust. She teaches at the Sorbonne and also in a couple of the American college programs for study abroad. I got the impression that his was the real academic career. She seems to be much more of a lightweight. Oh, I don't mean she's not accomplished. I just mean it appears that Albert was very well known not only in France but all over the world.'

Gilet had learned enough to dispel any doubt Corbet might have had about the identity of Marie Marceau.

'Did you happen to find out whether Albert knew François de La Roche?' Corbet tried to appear calmer than he felt.

'Yes, I believe Madame Marceau mentioned to me that she had heard about the death of de La Roche. She mentioned that he and Albert had just become acquainted through their editor. Apparently they had the same one at Galliante.'

'What will it be, sir?' Jacques was inquiring of Gilet, who ordered the salade frisée with cheese, potatoes and bacon.

'Do you think there's any connection between the two deaths?' This time Corbet didn't hesitate to go right to the point.

'Well, it seems kind of strange that they were both killed in what looks like the same way. Ménager says that even though all of the tests aren't back on Albert, he's almost certain it was cyanide in tea that killed him.'

'Yes, that's what I was afraid of. What were the men able to retrieve from the scene of the Albert death, the restaurant?' Corbet took a large bite of his omelette and waited for Gilet's reply.

'Well, he was drinking tea and eating madeleines when he died. But there was no poison found in the crumbs. It seems to have been confined to the tea. It was found in the tea in the bottom of the cup.' Gilet seemed to be trying not to let the topic of conversation interfere with his enjoyment of his salad.

'How could anyone have gained entry to the kitchen of the restaurant to have done the poisoning?' Corbet inquired, resolving to go and check out the scene himself very soon.

'Well, you see there's a back door off the courtyard where all of the apartments are. Also, Marie Marceau and Albert were the only customers in the restaurant at that time. It was late, around 10.30 p.m., and they were the only ones.' Gilet was eager to tell all he knew.

'You mean the same courtyard that contains the entrance to the de La Roche apartment?'

'Yes, I'm afraid so,' Gilet added.

'It might have been an inside job. Did anyone at the restaurant see a person who didn't belong there around the time of Albert's death?'

'No one saw anyone, but the Albert tray was left unattended for a bit before being brought to the table, and the waiter who was serving them said that he remembers now noticing that the door to the courtyard was left slightly ajar. He swears he didn't see anyone, however.' Gilet had finished his salad.

'Jacques, what time do you close here?' Corbet inquired of the proprietor of Le Blason.

'Oh, eleven, usually. Midnight on Saturday nights. Why? You want to come late at night? I don't make omelettes late at night, you know,' he said with sunny conviviality.

'Oh, I know that, Jacques. I was just wondering if you had noticed anybody unusual coming in here on Saturday night – anyone, I mean, other than the regulars. Anyone you didn't know or who seemed a little strange?' Corbet was not optimistic that he would turn anything up.

'Let me see. Saturday. Saturday. Oh, yes. The Benoîts were here earlier in the evening. They had a quarrel and left. Not very pleasant. Let me see. Yes, yes. There was a man who came in late, around eleven, eleven-thirty. He seemed out of place. I could have sworn he didn't live in Paris. Looked fresh from the provinces. Seemed a little rattled. Ordered a couple of cognacs and drank them right down, one right after another.'

'Did he say anything to you?' Corbet pressed.

'No, other than to order the drinks, nothing.'

'Very good. I'll head back to the Préfecture now and see what other reports have come in. I must speak with Leroux about his interview with the people around Albert's death. Do you know anything else?'

'Not really. I think Leroux has also spoken with Marie Marceau, but what he found out, I don't know.'

Corbet looked intently at the last piece of food on his plate before putting it into his mouth. He swallowed his last gulp of wine, and a shiver of dread mixed with anticipation ran down his back.

Chapter Ten

Inspector Corbet made his way back to his office at the Quai des Orfèvres through the large room full of desks of subordinates. He nodded at a few people as he passed by but clearly gave off the message that he was in no mood to chat or pass the time of day. No one tried to persuade him otherwise. He entered his office, took off his coat and hung it up.

The omelette was not settling well. He had eaten it too fast. He looked around for a cup into which to pour some mineral water to aid his digestion. Gulping the water, he cast his eyes across his desk and noticed a note from Leroux. He reached for the phone and dialled his extension.

'Corbet here. What else did you find out from the Marceau woman?'

'Oh, yes, Inspector. She really wants to talk to you.'

'Really?' Corbet didn't want to let on how much he, too, wanted to talk to her. 'I'll call her and arrange for an interview. Maybe I can get something else.'

'I hope so. She seemed to know you and asked some questions about your past which I couldn't answer.'

'Well, I'll speak with her.' Corbet volunteered nothing further.

He hung up the receiver and reached for a Paris phone directory, found the number he sought and dialled.

'*Allô.*' The voice was soft and sedate and that of a woman.

'This is Inspector Henri Corbet calling. I'd like to speak with Marie Marceau.' Corbet wanted to make no assumptions.

'Oh, Henri, yes, this is Marie. Remember me? We were students together at the Sorbonne.' Her unguarded friendliness worked to disarm Corbet.

'Why, Marie, of course. My God, it's been a long time, hasn't it? I've lost touch with my colleagues in the academic world. This is really a different world here.'

Corbet was reluctant to get too close to the real reason for his initial loss of contact with Marie.

'I'm sorry we're meeting again under these circumstances.' Marie sighed, and the lightness seemed to slip out of her tone. 'I still can't believe what has happened.'

'Well, why don't we get together and talk about it. Do you want to meet for lunch tomorrow?' Corbet needed a little time to prepare himself for re-entry into the past.

'Fine. My classes end at one o'clock. Why don't you meet me at the Jockey, around the corner from the Bryn Mawr College headquarters.'

'Certainly. The Jockey. Haven't been there in a while. Do they still have a good plat du jour?' Corbet remembered eating the most delightful eggs florentine the last time he was there.

'Yes, as a matter of fact, they do. They have wonderful stuffed vegetables. Most of the students have left by one o'clock, and we can lunch in relative quiet.'

'See you there.' He hung up the receiver. How long had it really been since he had seen Marie? Probably twenty-five years at least, maybe more.

It was true that one of the reasons he had lost touch with her was because their worlds had become very different when he left academia to do police work. It was an odd jump to make. Most people didn't do that. No one in his family had done police work. He was supposed to become a lawyer like his father. However, he had been able to persuade his parents to let him study history for a while and earn a Licence before going to study the law.

He had also taken the opportunity to take as many literature courses as he could. He had been fascinated by Dostoyevsky's observation of crime and various forms of transgression. It showed man on the edge and provided a glimpse into the drama of the human soul. He wanted to know more about that part of mankind in the twentieth century. Police work seemed to be a way to get there. His family was mortified. He was breaking a long tradition and stepping down in the world in their eyes. They were never the same with him.

Chapter Eleven

The Métro ride to the Tuileries didn't take too long and gave Corbet a chance to sort himself out after his conversation with Marie.

The rue de Castiglione was quiet for this time of day. He headed for the rue du Mont Thabor but decided to keep going to the rue Saint Honoré, to the chocolate shop. His office supply was nearly depleted. He selected two one-pound boxes of assorted chocolates and a pound of chocolate truffles, paid for them and went out into the street again.

He hadn't bothered to phone Rachel Todd first. It was late enough in the afternoon that there was a good chance she would be home from her classes.

Coming back from his purchase and once again approaching the grand wooden doors at 37 rue du Mont Thabor, he was relieved to see that one of the door panels stood open and that there was a clear path to the elevator past the little house of the concierge.

Up again he went in the small elevator. He knocked on the door he knew to be that of the studio and waited for a response. None came. He knocked again and waited. Nothing. He would have to make sure he called the next time he tried to talk to her. Turning and walking straight across the hall, he knocked at the door of the de La Roche apartment. No answer. He knocked again. He could hear someone heading to the door from what sounded like the back of the apartment. He waited.

'Who's there?' a woman's voice inquired. He didn't recognise the voice.

'Inspector Corbet, Paris Police.' He waited for the door to open. When it did, he was faced with a plump woman who held a rag in her hand. She had obviously been cleaning the apartment.

'May I speak to someone in the de La Roche family?' Corbet wasn't too hopeful that he would have any luck.

'One moment, please.' The woman went to the back of the apartment and entered a room. Pierre came out of the room in a dressing-gown, looking as though he had just been awakened from a nap.

'Oh, Inspector Corbet, forgive me. I've been so upset by all of the recent events. I haven't been sleeping. I thought I might get some sleep this afternoon. No luck.' Pierre seemed glad to have someone to talk to.

Corbet inquired about the whereabouts of Rachel Todd and was told that she had left Paris for a long weekend. She had left an address and a telephone number where she could be reached in an emergency. Pierre fumbled in a desk drawer and came up with a slip of paper on which was written the phone number of the Abbey of Saint Wandrille.

'She went down there with her boyfriend. He does research on churches, on French churches or something like that. She said she needed to get out of the city for a while. Can't say I blame her, but don't know that I would have chosen a monastery myself. In any case, she can be reached there.'

'When did she say she would return?' Corbet didn't want any more unnecessary delay in this case.

'Oh, after the weekend, sometime next week.' Pierre seemed very cheerful.

'Thank you.' Corbet closed the door behind him. It wouldn't do to wait that long. He would have to go out to the abbey near Rouen. It was only an hour by train from Paris. He would do it after he talked to Marie.

When he got out into the street, he opened one of his boxes of Marquise de Sévigné chocolates and helped himself to a couple of choice morsels. A finger of guilt needled the *bien-être* which he felt from his chocolate fix. He had to get to Galliante to talk with Monsieur Simon.

First he took the Métro to the Saint Michel stop and exited on to the Boulevard Saint Michel. He turned the corner by Gibert Jeune, the gigantic corner bookstore, in order to take a peek at Notre Dame. Since the Préfecture was so close to the cathedral he did this often, always feeling a sense of wonder upon beholding this large, grey, imposing landmark. He loved her.

He retraced his steps and headed down the Boulevard Saint Michel. He realised it had been years since he'd revisited the grand amphitheatre at the Sorbonne where he used to attend lectures on history and literature. A melancholy nostalgia led him to that courtyard where he had often spoken with Marie and the other students in his classes. Today it was filled with young people, very young people, it seemed. He felt a bit out of place but proceeded to enter the building.

He opened the large double doors of an entry to the circular lecture hall. It hadn't really changed in all these years. Here were the same wooden benches all circling around the stage where the lecturer held forth.

He glanced up into the balcony to where he used to sit. He could hear Professor Truchet lecturing on the nineteenth-century novel and see the curls gently lying on Marie's shoulders in the row down in front.

A chill in the air from the late afternoon cooling down of the building brought him around. He exited the court yard again and headed out to the boulevard, deciding to take the long walk from there to the Quai Voltaire, to the rue du Bac and on to the rue Sébastien-Bottin.

Chapter Twelve

The editor's office was on the fourth floor, way in the back. The building dated from the seventeenth century, and the small but high-ceilinged rooms had not been altered or remodelled. In a small entryway before Monsieur Simon's office was a desk occupied by a very alert-looking young woman dressed in what Corbet was sure must be the latest fashion. Her severe but well-shaped haircut and well-manicured nails spoke of someone who took great pride in her personal appearance.

Corbet showed her his identification and asked to speak with the editor. She nodded affirmatively and knocked on the door to the office, was let in, entered and closed the door. Opening the door again, she motioned for Corbet to enter.

The room was small and dominated by a large desk in the centre. Every inch of space was used for storing books, manuscripts, or piles of papers. Behind the desk sat a very large, angular, dark-haired man who Corbet guessed must be very tall, judging from the length of the arm he held across the desk to greet him.

'René Simon. Do sit down, Inspector.' Corbet looked at the only other chair in the room, which was piled high with books. Monsieur Simon started to come from behind the desk to remove them when Corbet reassured him that he could do so himself and did, placing them on the floor.

As he adjusted his solid form in the rather small wooden chair, Corbet eyes remained on Simon's elegant, angular face. His long, gallic nose was softened a bit by his almost shoulder-length black hair. His masculine and yet refined handsomeness made Corbet uncomfortable. He reached up to straighten his straw and silver hair with both hands and imagined his chin an inch longer and his jowls less heavy. His imagination failed him, and he felt like a bulky, rugged-looking, middle-aged man who had no chic and no style, whose good soul was invisible.

'Yes, Inspector, what can I do for you?' Simon broke Corbet's silence. Corbet removed his hands from his head, adjusted the sleeves of his jacket, which was beginning to feel much too tight, and dove into his interrogation.

'Yes, Monsieur Simon, I appreciate your taking the time to talk with me this afternoon. I came by on the chance that you might accommodate me, and I thank you in advance for your time.'

'Certainly. No problem. How may I assist you, Inspector? I assume you're here about the Albert and de La Roche deaths?'

'But of course, Monsieur, I am. I understand that you were the editor for the soon-to-be-published memoirs of the late François de La Roche?'

'I was. It was going to be quite a book. We wanted to get it out within the year because of the public interest in firsthand accounts of that time. Also, François wasn't getting any younger. We were making excellent progress on it, but as you know, now there may be some delay if the rights to the book get tied up in post-mortem legal tangles.'

'Yes, I can imagine that might cause some difficulty.' Corbet seized the verbal floor to continue. 'Can you tell me, were you having any difficulty with de La Roche in terms of his co-operating with you to get the book finished?'

'Difficulty? What do you mean by difficulty? François was a very particular, meticulous man and insisted that everything be as completely accurate as possible. He always wanted to double check everything before finalising a chapter.' Simon didn't seem to want to discuss the difficulties which were reported to Corbet by Madame de La Roche.

'Well, what about the contents of the book, the memoirs? Memoirs are memories, remembrances of things past. Was there a problem with de La Roche's memory? Was it too selective or too comprehensive?'

'As I said, François was very, very thorough. He had kept detailed journals throughout his career. He was unlikely to leave anything out.' Simon held one slender hand with another on top of the desk. A small diamond ring on his left little finger gleamed in the late afternoon light which came from the small, high window over his head. Its hard, shining elegance complemented that of its wearer. Corbet stared at his own hefty, ringless fingers.

'Was this tendency towards thoroughness a problem for an editor? I mean, did you find that he wanted to include too much?' Corbet took his eyes from his fingers and stared into Simon's midnight blue eyes. Simon shifted in his seat, unfolded his hands and leaned forward, his sharp chin on one of his slender hands.

'Well, an editor is always cutting here and there, always tightening. That's our job. It often seems to the writer that we are merciless surgeons with never dulling scalpels, but, really, it's necessary. One often can't see oneself what needs to be trimmed, what's redundant, what's inappropriate.' Simon checked himself and shifted his whole weight in the chair on that last word.

'What do you mean by *inappropriate*?' Corbet closed in. 'What's inappropriate about someone's memory of past events, about the events in his own life?'

'Perhaps that's the wrong word. I should say more to the point not in good taste.' Simon smoothed back his shiny black hair with his other long hand.

'By that I mean – well, you see, as you know, François was a member – or maybe you didn't know. At any rate, François was a member of the Vichy government during the Second World War. Much of what went on during those times under that regime is just now coming to light. François wanted to be an important part of the enlightenment of the French public.

'However, the present-day conservative faction of the government has an interest in not having too much exposed, and neither it nor the left-wing, more liberal faction wants anything brought to light which would tarnish the myth of the Resistance. So, there you have it.' Simon leaned back in his chair and stretched both long arms out in front of him, folding his hands as though in prayer.

Corbet struggled to digest this cool assessment of every good reason to censor the truth. 'But what about what really did happen? Aren't the people entitled to know that?'

'I suppose they will eventually learn of it, but those in authority had hoped that it would happen later, after all of those involved had been dead for a while and when the country had a new focus, some new triumphs to cushion the blows to the national pride that this would cause.'

Corbet considered himself a Frenchman to the core but had always been puzzled by this arrogant sense of nationalism and pride which afflicted his countrymen, which had led to the Vichy government's complicity with the Germans as well as to the glorification of De Gaulle as the saviour of free France.

He couldn't deny that without the aid of the Americans, France would never have been liberated. Why his fellow Frenchmen had so much trouble acknowledging that had always escaped him. Only a visit to the American Cemetery in Normandy with its rows and rows of white, often anonymous, crosses testified to that. The French had a debt to America that they seemed only backhandedly able to acknowledge.

'It's a pity that pride demands such denial,' Corbet said flatly. 'But de La Roche wanted to change all of this and tarnish the image, I gather, and, therefore, you were urging him not to do something so, as you said, *inappropriate*? Is that it?'

'Sort of. As an editor, there's much that I have to consider when deciding to publish a book. The house can't risk publishing something that's going to be too unfavourably received by too many people. That's just the business of publishing. In some sense, we must give the people what they want to read. We can't force the truth on them if they aren't ready to hear it.' Simon seemed removed from the words he was uttering.

'Or to pay for it may be more to the point,' Corbet punctured Simon's flat delivery.

'Well, yes, that too,' Simon conceded.

'But I understand that de La Roche was really resisting your efforts at censoring his work?' Corbet pressed.

'He was. We had many long discussions about it. François's strong personal need to confess what he considered his wrongdoing and complicity by revealing that of the whole Vichy government had become an obsession with him. He carried a lot of guilt about his first family. His wife was taken by the Germans in spite of his high connections in the government.

'There is a scene which François describes in the memoirs – one of the questionable scenes, obviously – where he tells of his visit to Château des Sources, then occupied by the Germans, to discuss the possible liberation of his wife and the fate of his son. He's told that she must go to Poland to a camp and that his son can be deported to England if he is willing to finance it. It's a very moving piece of writing, but we weren't going to be able to include it. François was adamant that it should go in the book. I tried to persuade him otherwise. We were at a standstill on this major issue as well as many minor points throughout the work.'

'When he died, he was on his way to Paris to visit with you. Was this what you were going to discuss if he had made the meeting?' Corbet inquired.

'Oh, most definitely. And François had also intimated on the phone that he had come to some decision and needed to talk to me. Needless to say, I was eagerly awaiting my interview with him.'

'I'm sure you were.' Simon was beginning to annoy Corbet. He seemed as sly in his more polished and sophisticated manner as Pierre had in his oily and unctuous way. He decided to head to the heart of the matter.

'François de La Roche died on a train from Bordeaux to Paris on Saturday night at around 8 p.m. Did he hope to meet with you on Saturday night when he got into Paris?'

'Oh, no. But first thing on Sunday. He had called me from Bordeaux on Saturday to tell me he needed to see me first thing Sunday morning. I suggested that we might wait until Monday morning, but he would have no part of it. He wanted to see me right away. He said it was rather urgent.'

'And you agreed?'

'But of course,' Simon countered.

'And then where were you on Saturday night when de La Roche was swallowing cyanide in a train car headed for Paris?' Corbet pressed.

'Oh, it was cyanide? You know that for sure?'

'We do now,' Corbet affirmed.

'Well, I was actually – you see, my wife was out of town at our place in the country, in Brittany. I was in town but not at my apartment. It's a little awkward.' Simon looked rather sheepishly at Corbet.

'So where were you?' Corbet felt merciless.

'Well, you see, I was with a friend, a friend who would not want you to know her name. There's no need to involve her. She has nothing to do with this. It would just really complicate matters.' Simon almost began to plead.

'But I must know who it is. I'll need to speak to her to confirm your story. Her name will be kept in confidence. Don't worry.' Corbet was determined to get the information from this handsome cur.

'All right. It's against my better judgement, but, if you must know, her name is Jacqueline, Jacqueline Champigneulle. She's a friend of Madame de La Roche's. In fact, I met her through Madame de La Roche.' Simon seemed relieved to end the struggle.

'Madame de La Roche? You mean, Thérèse de La Roche, François's wife?' Corbet was surprised at this connection.

'Yes, the very same. In fact, Thérèse and I are good friends, at least now we are. At one time, it was something a little different. But this was before I began to have business dealings with François. It was all finished by then. I was very fond of her, but she seemed unwilling to get attached to anyone. And, believe me, it was not out of love for François. I mean, she respected him, but that part of their relationship was over a long time ago. Thérèse was her own person. I fell pretty hard, and I think she was starting to when she called it off.'

Corbet could certainly understand how one could fall hard for Thérèse de La Roche. Thoughts of her were haunting him even while he pressed on with his investigations. He knew that he wouldn't even have the opportunity to be ultimately brushed off as Simon had been.

He couldn't get an opening shot under the present circumstances, but even if things were different – well, if things were different, she probably wouldn't even deign to speak to Inspector Henri Corbet of the Paris Police. So perverse is the attraction of one human being for another that he was almost glad for the unhappy chance to have become acquainted with her.

'I recovered my balance, and, almost as a peace offering, she introduced me to Jacqueline. She's a very attractive woman, a talented writer. Her husband was also busy with many things other than his relationship with his wife, and, so, we began to spend time together. However, she wouldn't want it publicised. It would just make things awkward. I'm sure you can understand, Inspector Corbet.' Simon was very persuasive.

'But of course I can understand,' Corbet assured him. 'However, I will have to speak with this woman. There's no way around that.'

'All right. But do be discreet,' urged Simon.

'I will,' Corbet promised. 'Thank you so much for your time, Mr. Simon. I must go now.' Corbet was glad of the formal ending of the interview. He had a lot to digest.

'You're welcome, Inspector. Anytime I can be of help, you know where to find me. I do hope you get to the bottom of this soon.'

'Oh, one more topic I neglected to cover.' Corbet had become a bit derailed by the knowledge of the connections between Simon and Thérèse de La Roche and had forgotten to probe Simon for his involvement with Albert.

'I must press on with a few more questions, Mr. Simon. I understand that François de La Roche was acquainted with Roger Albert, a man who was found dead in a restaurant after drinking some tea laced with cyanide.'

'Oh, yes. Poor Roger. His book on Proust was – still is – going to be the best produced to date. It's a literary biography of such breadth and depth that I doubt we'll have another like it for some time. He was one of France's leading academics. It's a great loss to all of us.' Simon finished his eulogy.

'So I understand. But what exactly was the relationship between Albert and de La Roche? Tell me what you know about it.'

'Well, I believe I introduced them. Galliante had a gathering, a sort of reception, if you will, for all of our new authors. That was about six months ago. It was there that they met. François indicated how impressed he was with Albert's work and his intellect. They often had dinner together. François seemed to get a strange sort of comfort from Albert.'

'I always thought it a rather odd connection. De La Roche was old enough to be Albert's father, and Albert seemed to be a much more literary fellow than François. At any rate, they found something in one another. Albert for his part was also taken with François. He seemed to like the attention of the older man. More than that, I cannot tell you.' Simon stretched his long arms across the desk and glanced up at Corbet, who was looking him right in the eyes.

'I imagine de La Roche had confided in Albert about his difficulties with the censorship of his book?' Corbet pressed.

'I can't really say. All I know is that Roger spoke to me once about how ironic it was that he could encounter no censure in revealing all the sordid details of Proust's sex life and yet François was having difficulties with his revelations of French complicity in the Vichy government. He certainly sympathised more with de La Roche's position than with that of Galliante.'

'Can you think of any other connections that might exist between de La Roche and Albert that might link these two deaths?'

'None other than what I've told you.' Simon seemed eager to get this over with. He said he had a dinner date with Jacqueline and didn't want to be late.

'Well, all right. Thank you very much. I'll be in touch.' Corbet put down the sword and left the offices of Galliante. He would have to make his own connections.

Chapter Thirteen

As he rode the Métro towards the Tuileries stop, Inspector Corbet felt very energised. He had decided to dine early at the Hotel Meurice on the rue de Rivoli. It had been the former headquarters of General von Choltitz of the Wehrmacht before the liberation of Paris. Corbet often ate in the restaurant of the hotel, but tonight the history of the Meurice took on a new poignancy.

Still reeling from his interview with Simon, he felt he needed some quiet time to think before moving further into this mass of tangled lives and motives that was opening up before him. Also, he had promised to visit his father later in the evening, and he could easily reach his house on the edge of the Bois de Boulogne by cab from the Hotel Meurice. Simon's mention of the Château des Sources had rung a bell. He remembered that his father had often spoken of a client he had who lived there.

As he entered the softly lit, ornately decorated dining-room, the maître d' recognised him and led him to the table he usually occupied for his early dinners. The waiter handed him the special, less formal menu for early dinners at the Meurice. Corbet ordered a half-bottle of Brouilly. That hearty red would be a good accompaniment to the steak au poivre and the gratin of potatoes he planned to order for dinner. He decided on an appetiser of escargots. Every now and then he craved snails.

As his fork pierced the first little creature and Corbet prepared to bring it to his mouth, he was suddenly overcome with a hushed horror at what de La Roche must have witnessed in the Vichy government. Here in this very hotel was stationed von Choltitz, who had been ordered by Hitler to prepare to defend Paris from the Allies and free French at all costs, even at the cost of blowing up its most precious monuments – Notre Dame, the Arc de Triomphe, the Opera, all the bridges over the Seine. My God, if von Choltitz had followed Hitler's insane orders, there would be no Paris as Corbet now knew and loved it. His beloved Notre Dame would be gone.

He put his fork down and decided to wait before beginning his meal. He took a long drink of Brouilly and settled back in his seat. The Préfecture of Police was one of the main targets for the proposed demolition, and even Corbet's headquarters would have been destroyed. It somehow seemed unimaginable that this had gone on in a civilised world in the middle of the twentieth century.

During the war Corbet had been a little boy and had spent most of the time in the South of France, near Nice, with his mother and relatives. His father had remained in Paris during the Occupation. Whenever Corbet questioned him about what had gone on, he would give evasive answers such as 'Everyone has his Vichy. It's very complicated.' The elder Corbet seemed pained at the mention of those times. Corbet had always had a great curiosity about exactly what had happened then, but he hesitated to try to force his father to talk about it. Much remained buried. It was brave of de La Roche to wish to excavate some of it. No wonder someone wanted him dead.

Corbet again picked up the first snail on his plate of escargots and popped it into his mouth. The heavy garlic, butter and parsley flavour surrounding the titbit burst in his mouth like a loud symphony. He never tired of the garlic surprise that accompanied each bite of the dish. He mopped up the butter sauce with a fresh piece of baguette and then followed the second snail with a long drink of the wine.

The thought that he was really going to see Marie again after all this time was just beginning to sink in. How would he feel about her now? Would the old magic still be there? In less than twenty-four hours he would know. How life could change in such a short time.

He began to wonder what de La Roche's last twenty-four hours had been like. He had obviously made some decision he wanted to discuss with Simon. His book could really be a time bomb that would blow a hole in the wall of denial so long cultivated by the authorities.

Funny about that denial. He had noticed it in Germany, too. When he was in Heidelberg, it was as though there had never been a Second World War. The young Germans were not even taught about it in school. Corbet had found that very odd and disconcerting. Yet it seemed the denial in his own country was equally pernicious.

The waiter removed his empty plate and prepared the area for the main course. Corbet's appetite had been whetted by the little snails, and he looked forward to the steak au poivre and gratin which would be followed by a simple green salad to cleanse his palate before dessert. When the waiter set the steak and gratin in front of him, Corbet readjusted his napkin and prepared to feast.

As he cut into the medium-rare morsel of steak covered with dark, cracked peppercorns, again the image of Marie as he had last seen her came before his eyes. She had been so very attractive then.

As he bit into the snappy, peppery morsel, he recalled his recent encounter with Thérèse de La Roche. She was indeed a haunting woman. There was something inherently evasive about her, and it was that that disturbed him. There was much more there than would ever meet the eye, he was sure, and he wondered how he was going to get to the bottom of it all. He was certain that she had only given him the top layer of some muffled version of the truth.

The gratin was hot and soothing. The potatoes were cooked to perfection and added hearty support to the steak. When his taste buds were pleased Corbet was usually a happy man, but tonight he felt agitated, somehow on edge. Too many things from the past were resurfacing too rapidly. He knew that life had a way of moving inexorably forward and suspected that if he were to try too hard to go back to things as they had been, the changes in him alone created by the movement of time would extinguish any real hope of beginning again with Marie after all of these years. Look what had happened to de La Roche when he had wanted to excavate the past merely to say how it had been. The peppery steak was disappearing rapidly as Corbet chewed on these weighty matters.

When the waiter came to take his dessert order, Corbet put down the card and ordered a strawberry tart. He began to brace himself for the meeting with his father. It was about once a month that he made the trip out to the old family home on the edge of the Bois de Boulogne. His mother had been dead for about eight years. His father's health and mental state had been in a decline since her passing.

Theirs had been a workable marriage, maybe even a good marriage, as marriages go. Corbet had never been subjected to being put in the middle of two warring camps, as so often happened in families where there was marital discord and an only child. His parents had always presented what he perceived to be a united front in terms of their view of his life and activities.

They had both been disappointed when he had chosen the life of a police inspector – his father because his son would not become eligible to work with him in his law practice, his mother because she didn't want her son involved in such dangerous work, and both of them because of the inferior social status implied by the nature of the work. Corbet had stood his ground. He felt that as time went on they had become more tolerant of his chosen life, but they could never embrace it.

And, so, there was always a reserve in his relationship with his parents, a reserve that had become greater with his father since the death of his mother. Nonetheless, Corbet had felt a sense of duty to keep up the visits and to try to maintain what his father would allow of the father-son relationship.

Chapter Fourteen

The cab drew up to a rather imposing grey structure, the Corbet family home. His father had been quite successful in his law practice, and the family had lived the life of *la grande bourgeoisie.*

Corbet rang the bell, was admitted by his father's butler and led into the impressive, book-lined library where his father was seated in a chair near the large marble fireplace.

As Corbet made his way towards him, Julien Corbet rose slightly in his chair as though to come to meet him, but Henri motioned for him to remain seated, gave his coat to the butler and took the chair on the other side of the fireplace. He sat for a moment just looking at his father. Even though it had only been a month since he had seen him, he appeared more frail than he had on the last visit.

Julien Corbet was a tall, raw-boned man with a great shock of long white hair. It was obvious that it was from him that Corbet had gotten his large, gallic nose and features. Corbet suppressed a little shudder when he noticed how his father was yet again thinner. Julien Corbet's gaunt figure suggested something otherworldly, something ghost-like, as though the shell were being vacated ever so gradually by some sort of spiritual wasting. Henri felt his heart twist, and he checked himself from attempting to embrace his father. The tenderness came out in his tone when he spoke to him.

'Well, Father, shall we have a little Courvoisier to take the chill off?' His father nodded in agreement, and the butler headed for the cabinet to get the decanter and the glasses. Corbet received the large round glass of brown liquid with gratitude.

'The papers are full of the de La Roche and Albert murders. I suppose you're assigned to them?' His father took a long drink from his glass and gazed strongly at Henri.

'Yes, as a matter of fact I am, Father.' Julien Corbet normally didn't take such an interest in his son's work, but the victims in these cases were simply too well known for him to avoid any talk of it. Corbet found that he was perversely grateful for the notoriety of the cases. He wanted to talk with his father about them, and it would be easier now since he had at least shown some initial interest.

'They're turning into quite a puzzle. I'm not at liberty to disclose too much of what I'm doing, as you know, but I do need to ask you a few questions since it's possible you might know something that would be helpful to me.'

Julien Corbet moved his head forward as though to listen more carefully to what his son had to say. The wrinkles of loose skin on his neck were a reminder that the body of his father had once had much more bulk, a bulk not unlike his own. Inspector Corbet wondered whether he would become thin and frail like that in old age. He couldn't imagine himself without his girth.

'I'll do what I can, Henri. You know I will.' This was as close as his father would get to showing any warmth or tenderness towards him.

'I'll need to ask you some questions, and I can only give you a sketch of why. It seems that François de La Roche was a member of the Vichy government, and he was in the process of writing his memoirs.'

'Yes, *Le Monde* had a story on his background. There now seems to be some difficulty about whether the book will get published posthumously?' Julien Corbet took a large swallow of his drink.

'That's right. I've just talked to his editor, René Simon, about that very subject. There may be some difficulties. But there were difficulties even before the death of François de La Roche. It seems he was about to reveal some rather shocking truths about the behaviour of the Vichy govern-ment during the war as well as the behaviour of a lot of our countrymen.' Corbet took a small sip of his drink.

'You said the man's name was Simon?' Julien Corbet inquired with some interest.

'Yes, René Simon. He's one of the top editors for Galliante.

'Well, I wonder if he's related to Charles Simon, one of Vichy's prime collaborators? He was known as some sort of a local tyrant and emissary for Vichy.' Julien Corbet finished the last remarks and stared into the fireplace.

'I'm sure I don't know. I just met Mr Simon this even-ing. I haven't had a chance to check his background. Indeed, I didn't ask him anything about his past. I was more interested in his immediate involvement with de La Roche and Albert. But I'll certainly look into it.'

Corbet found that even the good belts of Courvoisier were not quelling his mounting agitation. He continued. 'I know that during the war I was in Nice with Grandmother and Grandfather, Mother and I were. But you were up here, and you may know something about what went on during that time that will be helpful to me.' Corbet drained his drink and put it down on the table beside the chair. He would think about whether to take a refill.

'Yes. I thought it best not to expose you and your mother to the goings-on here in Paris.'

'It's those *goings-on*, as you call them, that I need to know more about.' Corbet could feel his father begin to do his usual withdrawal on the subject. 'Father, I know this may not be pleasant for you, but I must ask some questions.

If you can possibly help me in solving these murders, I would be very grateful.' Corbet's eyes pleaded with him.

'I'll do what I can, Henri.' His father let a large sigh escape and leaned back in his chair. 'You know, the Paris Police were no angels in those days. They reported many Jews to the authorities who later had them deported and killed.'

'It seems that a lot was not as it should have been then. Can you help me?' The direct plea softened Julien Corbet. He leaned back in his chair and took a deep breath.

'I remember your telling me of a client of yours who lived in a château outside of Paris. I believe it was called Château des Sources.' Corbet waited.

'Well, as you know, I remained here in Paris working as much as I could during the Occupation. One of my clients was a Marquis Louis de Courcey who lived in a large château near Fontainebleau. I was their family lawyer, and before the war I would often visit Château des Sources. It was a magnificent, rambling old château.

'One of the things I used to enjoy most was the hunt weekends. Every autumn the Marquis de Courcey would invite me, along with a number of other people, for a long weekend of hunting and dining. It was my first real taste of how the aristocracy lived. I liked it very much. You would have appreciated the cuisine, Henri.' He looked his son in the eye. Corbet could have sworn there were tears in his father's eyes. He stood, went over to him and put his hand on his shoulder. The old man sat in silent acknowledgement of the gesture.

'Yes, it seems as though the war has changed many things, and there's an innocence we can never recapture. We keep feeling the loss.' Corbet gently removed his hand from his father's shoulder and took his seat again.

'Yes,' Julien Corbet continued, 'during the war the Marquis became very involved in the Resistance. The château was occupied by the Nazis, and he and his family were forced to turn their kitchen over to preparing meals for the German troops. De Courcey was very brave, though. He stood his ground and lived under what must have been almost intolerable circumstances.' Julien Corbet drained his glass and called for a refill. Corbet also held his glass out for the butler to refill.

'Did the Marquis confide in you while all of this was going on at his château?' Corbet took a long drink of the cognac.

'Yes. In retrospect, I believe I had a vicarious involvement with the Resistance through him. He told me many, many things about what went on then.'

'Well, François de La Roche mentioned Château des Sources in his memoirs as having been the place where he pleaded with the Nazis to grant him some kind of immunity for his wife. He had hoped that his position with the Vichy government would help him. It didn't, and his wife was carted off. He was able to negotiate a bit over the fate of his son, who was sent to England. Those were terrible times.' Corbet watched as his father lowered his head and seemed to get lost in his own thoughts. He sat in silence and waited.

Julien Corbet looked up and gazed into his son's eyes. 'Henri, I can't imagine how I could have gone on living if I had lost your mother that way, if they had taken you to England. That must have been unbearable for him.' He shifted his gaze towards the burning logs in the fireplace.

'That's why he needed so desperately to write his memoirs and have them published. It's as though he didn't want to live with the weight of the shadow of the past anymore.'

'Are you still in contact with anyone at Château des Sources?' Corbet had to get down to business.

'As a matter of fact, I am. I do keep in touch with Marquis Philippe de Courcey, the son of Louis. He took over the château when it was finally returned to the de Courcey family after the war. That took some time, however. First it was occupied by the Nazis, then used as an American prison camp, and then occupied by Field Marshall Montgomery, who was a guest there for some time.

'Philippe and his family have done a lot of restoration work and are quite happy living there now. Occasionally I get an invitation to spend the weekend with them. I haven't done so, however, for some time.' Julien Corbet finished his drink and placed his glass on the table beside his chair. He looked very tired, and Corbet knew he had to begin to wind up his visit.

'Father, do you think you could get me an invitation to the château? I would very much like to talk with the Marquis.' He waited for his father to respond.

'Well, Henri, you know that Philippe was only a little boy when all of this went on. He would have no real firsthand knowledge.' Corbet knew his father would really rather remain uninvolved in this, but he sat in silence.

Finally, Julien Corbet said, 'Very well. I'll call the Marquis and get you an interview as soon as possible. I'll have to tell him that it's not a social call, that you are on business.' He said the last word as though it left a bad taste in his mouth.

'But of course,' was all Henri replied. Julien motioned for the butler and asked that the telephone be brought over to him. The butler headed towards him trailing the long cord, and Henri decided to leave the room while his father made the call. He descended to the kitchen.

After speaking with Antoine, his father's long-time cook, and giving Julien Corbet what he felt was enough time to have a private conversation with the Marquis, Henri Corbet returned to the library where his father sat staring into the fire and waiting.

'Tomorrow evening, if you wish, you may go down to Château des Sources. The Marquise has insisted that you stay to dine. I think you should at least do that if you possibly can.' He still didn't take his gaze from the logs in the fireplace.

Henri Corbet approached his father's chair and again put his hand on his shoulder. 'Of course I will, Father.'

Chapter Fifteen

Sloane Hall was an eighteenth-century building on the rue de Chevreuse around the corner from the Jockey. It housed the administrative offices for several study abroad programs of America's more prestigious colleges and universities. It was in this building that Corbet was to find Valérie Ribeau the next morning. He entered the double doors and spoke to the concierge, who occupied a cage to the left, inquiring where he might find the offices of Bryn Mawr College and, in particular, a Valérie Ribeau. Fourth floor he was told, right over there.

There was no elevator, and so he had to climb all four flights of the narrow stairs. His accumulated bulk made it a rather laborious effort, reminding him of his age. He reached the top of the stairs on the fourth floor rather breathless and paused a moment to recover. At least the exertion diverted his attention from his anxiety over the upcoming reunion with Marie. He had not slept well last night. He wondered what would come of this, what he would find out about her, how he would react. He hoped he would be able to concentrate on his interview with Valérie Ribeau enough to get what he needed.

He knocked at the small white door to her office and was answered with a curt invitation to enter. When he did, he was faced immediately with a rather grey woman seated behind a desk. She was about sixty years of age. Her hair was grey. Her skin was grey, and she had a sour expression which seemed etched into her face.

'Madame Ribeau, is it?' He inquired gingerly.

'Mademoiselle,' she replied in a clipped, acerbic tone. 'What can I do for you?' Her tone said she didn't want to do anything for anybody.

'Henri Corbet, Paris Police. I'm here to discuss the recent deaths of François de La Roche and Roger Albert. Not a very pleasant topic, I know.' Corbet felt he needed to keep paving the way in order to get anywhere with this woman.

'Oh, yes. Such a horror. It's had me quite beside myself.' She became more human. 'I haven't been able to sleep well or concentrate since I got the news.'

'I understand that Monsieur de La Roche was your brother-in-law?' Corbet was somewhat distracted by the faint smell of stale tobacco that permeated the office.

'Why, yes, he was. My sister Hélène married him more years ago than I care to count. She's dead, too, you know. The Germans had her deported. First she went to Holland and then to Poland to die in a camp. She was young and quite beautiful. I was the less attractive one. I never married.' She eyed Corbet somewhat cautiously but seemed glad to have the chance to talk to somebody about the memories these events had stirred in her.

Corbet, welcoming the chance once again to be the recipient of any information to fill in the puzzle, eyed her calmly before his next question.

'She was of Jewish extraction then, I take it, as are you?'

'Yes. During the war I was hidden by a family who lived in Paris. They all but adopted me as their own.

'The family feared more for my safety than that of Hélène. She seemed so well-connected, being married to François and all. That proved no shield, however. He was forced to yield her to those German dogs.' Her eyes narrowed and her sour expression hardened into something more threatening and bitter.

Corbet averted his eyes to deflect the strong feelings that were coming from Valérie Ribeau. 'She had a son?' He pulled the question out of the air.

'Yes, she did. His name was Gerard. I'm not exactly sure what happened to him. I know he left France. I don't think he went to a camp, though. It's possible that he went along with many other children of Jewish origin to England. That was often an option that was given to parents with connections. I was very fond of him and felt his loss. You see, I have no children of my own.' She seemed to grow somewhat distracted.

'For me, Pierre has been a rather poor substitute for Gerard, I must say, and, it appears, for François, too. I think he felt that even though Thérèse was from the old aristocracy and, therefore, Pierre would be of purer blood than Gerard, that Pierre simply wasn't as gifted. I know he found him a disappointment. And I know that Pierre felt this, too. He seemed to take a perverse joy in disappointing his father, all the while playing the victim.' This woman was a better psychologist than Corbet would have given her credit for being.

'Do you know anything about the present whereabouts of Gerard?' He needed to keep moving.

'Well, I didn't until yesterday. I've never heard from him myself. When my family died, they left me very well provided for, and I've remained here since the war.' She seemed to want to tell her story.

'What happened yesterday?' Corbet was getting impatient.

'Pierre told me that he had learned of Gerard's whereabouts in London and that Rachel Todd, an American student who has rented the de La Roche studio, was his girlfriend. He said that he had met Gerard in London but had not told him of their relationship to one another. He certainly went out of his way to fix it so Rachel Todd would get the studio.' She took a deep breath.

'When I found this out, I was very angry. I felt as though he had used me. He, of course, didn't care. He never does about other people. He's always up to his own tricks. He's repulsive and seems to feel that just because he has a close and twisted relationship with his mother, he's somehow anointed.' She seemed only to be getting started on her diatribe against Pierre.

'Just what do you know about that relationship?' Corbet had to take some control.

'Well, I know that Thérèse is a cold and calculating woman who didn't take it too kindly when her only offspring was spurned by his father, François de La Roche.' Valérie Ribeau's mouth twisted anxiously and she picked up a pencil and began to chew on the end of it.

'What kind of contact, if any, did you have with François de La Roche?' Corbet needed to know this.

'Well, not much. He had always been a remote snob, and I don't think he ever really liked me. But things got worse after Hélène died. He seemed extremely uncomfortable around me after that and tried to minimise the contact. Not that I was seeking him out or anything. But we used to get together on some holidays and things like that. It was as if he had never really known me.' She reached up and patted her grey, frizzled hair.

'He did continue to list his studio apartment with me, though, and I have often found him foreign student tenants for that. I keep in marginal contact with his second wife, Thérèse. As I said, she's a rather distant and strange woman. Pierre, however, most often lets me know when the studio will be vacant. Some years they don't want to rent it at all.' Valérie was eyeing Corbet very carefully, and he was certain that she noticed his reaction to the mention of Thérèse de La Roche.

'And one of the students you rented to recently is this American student named Rachel Todd?' Corbet needed to continue.

'Yes. Pierre recommended her. He seems to have contacts everywhere. She's a graduate student in the Bryn Mawr program.'

Corbet wondered why Pierre seemed to be cropping up everywhere. 'How did he know she would be a student in the program?'

'He met her in London. He knows a lot of foreign students. They seem to amuse him. He also knew that Thérèse had been very disappointed with the last Bryn Mawr student I had placed in the studio. It seems she left quite a mess. Perhaps Pierre felt that if he found the right student his mother would be inclined to continue renting the studio to foreign students. God knows, Thérèse doesn't need the money. But I think there may be some arrangement with Pierre whereby he gets the rent fees as some kind of an allowance. He doesn't work, you know. Never has.'

'What does he do?' Corbet asked the next logical question.

'I think he just hangs around the apartment and looks after his mother. François didn't spend much time with them, you know. He was always busy with a project. Pierre has always been rather sickly. Rumour has it that he has had serious mental problems. What they are or were, I don't know.' Valérie Ribeau seemed to take pleasure in discussing other people's misfortunes and limitations.

'What do you know about Roger Albert?' Corbet pressed on.

'I know that he was found dead in a restaurant where he was having dinner with Marie Marceau. She's one of our professors here. We have a number of regular Sorbonne professors who teach our graduate students. I know that

Marie had some sort of long-standing relationship with this Albert and that he was working on a book about Proust. Marie seemed to feel he was spending too much time on it. That's all I know.' She seemed to be looking for closure now. Corbet wasn't. He needed to get to the most important part of his questioning.

'The night that de La Roche died on the train and Albert died in the restaurant, what were you doing? That would be Saturday night between eight and eleven o'clock.'

'Why, I was at home. I can't really remember what I was doing. Let's see. I was – Oh, now, what was I doing?' She seemed genuinely flustered and continued to register surprise that he should be asking her questions such as these.

'Why do you want to know about me?' she demanded, her harsh tone returning.

'I have to ask everyone who could possibly have any interest at all in seeing any of these people dead about his or her whereabouts. It's my job.'

'But you don't really think that I had anything to do with these deaths?' Valérie inquired of him with a severe, quizzical look.

'I don't know who had anything to do with them. That's what I'm trying to find out.' Corbet was beginning to get annoyed with her. 'I just want to know what you can tell me about your whereabouts that evening. That's all.'

'Well, I'm afraid I can't tell you very much. I know I was at home. My cat was sick on Saturday, and I had to take him to the veterinarian. I was at home nursing him. I was probably reading or watching television. That's the best I can do.' She seemed discouraged.

'Is there anybody whom you saw or spoke to that evening who would remember having seen or spoken to you?'

'No, not really. I was alone. I spoke with a friend earlier in the day, but that's it.' She seemed resigned now to her defenceless position.

'Well, I may have to talk with you further before this business is finished. I thank you for your time.'

Corbet was glad to close the interview. As he walked down the narrow hall and headed for the stairs, his anxiety over his encounter with Marie reappeared in the form of heavy breathing which had nothing to do with his descent of the stairs.

Chapter Sixteen

Corbet took the stairs at a good clip and was in the front hall passing by the concierge before he knew it. He became conscious of the fact that he was hurrying and told himself to slow down. The Jockey was only around the corner. He was a little early. It was only ten to one. He slowed his pace as he turned down the rue de Chevreuse and headed toward the Boulevard Montparnasse.

He would get there first and order some wine to calm his nerves before he encountered Marie. Rounding the corner on the Boulevard Montparnasse, he saw the sign, Le Jockey.

Upon entering through the brass-handled doors he noticed that the crowd was thinning. Marie had been right. The students were returning to classes, leaving behind only the lingering clouds of their cigarette smoke. He hoped it would clear before they ate. Too much of it might ruin his appetite, and he was uncertain as to how much he was going to be able to enjoy his meal anyway. Normally, being upset or excited didn't interfere with his ability to appreciate good food. He hoped that would be the case today. He noticed that the plat du jour was tomatoes stuffed with an herb-scented rice reminiscent of his youth in Provence.

He entered the large room full of red velveteen seats and booths surrounded by brass railings and lit by lily-shaped milk-glass lamps. As he sat down in one of the comfortable, red-cushioned booths for two, he could easily see young Marcel Proust and some of his friends gathering here for an apéritif in the afternoon. Settling into the seat which was just a bit too tight for his bulk, he waited for the waiter to approach. When he did, he ordered a half-bottle of Pomerol. He usually didn't drink much during the day, but this was a special occasion.

The taste of this rich red wine took him back to Bordeaux and his interview with Thérèse de La Roche. The last time a woman had had that kind of hypnotic effect on him it had been Marie in his student days at the Sorbonne. But with Marie he hadn't had the same instinctual reservations he had with Thérèse de La Roche. He remembered living for the classes in which he could look at her from the balcony and waiting to speak with her at breaks and after class.

While he felt that she liked him, seemed to enjoy discussing the lectures with him, and had even gone for coffee with him at a café on the Boulevard Saint Michel, he was certain in his deepest heart that she viewed him only as a friend. This, however, didn't stop his fancy from construing situations in which he would eventually win her love and spend his life with her.

The news of her engagement and subsequent marriage to the Italian noble had come as a shock, and he had gone into a rather flat depression for a long time after that. It was then that he decided he would not pursue a career in academia. He didn't really want to teach, and he was no scholar. While his interest in literature and history was genuine and came from some inner place, he couldn't seem to fashion it into a career. The law was out. He didn't want to live as his father had, from case to case, opportunity to opportunity. No. He needed something different.

It was in the semester after Marie's marriage that he had decided to spend a year studying abroad, one semester in Germany at the University of Heidelberg and the other at Pushkinski Dom in Leningrad. He had a rudimentary knowledge of both languages and was sure the exposure to life in the countries would sharpen his skills. That year was the loneliest of his life and yet the richest. He was able to get a window on to two very different cultures, very different from his own as well as from each other. The experience had changed him forever.

Sipping the wine and musing on his past, he was startled when he noticed an attractive woman standing by the side of his table holding out her hand to him.

'Henri, after all this time, I still recognise you!' Marie seemed genuinely glad to see him.

'Ah, Marie, do sit down. Yes, yes. It's wonderful to see you again.' He noticed how young she looked, how beautiful she still was. The wine had calmed his anxiety somewhat, and he hoped he appeared more self-possessed than he felt.

'It's terrible that we are meeting again under these circumstances.' Marie looked directly at him as she took her seat across from him.

'Ah, yes, it is. It's a nasty business. I'm sorry about your friend Albert.' Corbet felt he had to say this right away to remind himself of why he was here today, to forbid himself to slip into the past or to give her a chance to ask why he had just disappeared from her life, why he had never really said goodbye to her.

'Roger was a wonderful man. I loved him very much. Who would want to kill him? He was such a serious person, such a good scholar. I don't think I'll ever get over this.' Marie shifted her gaze from Corbet as she expressed her pain. He wanted to take her hand but restrained himself. She was still so lovely even in her sadness over another man.

'How long had you known Roger Albert?' Corbet needed to know these little details.

'I met him after I came back from Venice, after my divorce. He had been living with me for about three years. We were so happy at first, so very happy.' She seemed in danger of drifting off into some reverie about the beginning of her relationship with Albert. Corbet pulled her out of it.

'You weren't happy later, at the time of his death?' Corbet inquired.

'Well, we weren't unhappy. I was feeling very neglected. He was working so hard on his book on Proust and seemed preoccupied much of the time. I really felt left out. In fact, I had begun to wonder if he were involved with another woman, even though I was quite certain that his mistress was his work.' She paused for a minute.

'Sometimes I thought that was more difficult than if it had been another woman, because at least with another woman I could assess my competition and counter-attack. This way I could do nothing but stand by and wait for him to finish the book.' Corbet knew a lot about standing by and really could empathise with her. He still resisted taking her hand.

'Were there problems with the book? What had him so preoccupied?' He would need to know that.

'I'm not really sure. He was acting as though he might have something like writer's block, but I knew he didn't. He was a writer who could always write. I really think it was something other than the book that was bothering him, but I could never get him to tell me what it was. He would always say that he was worried about the book, about how it was going to be received, about whether he really would ever finish it. I knew that he would finish it and had no doubt that it would be very well received.'

'His editor, René Simon from Galliante, had been very pleased with the book and had indicated this to me when we went to a party for new authors at the house. In fact, it was then that I noticed Roger becoming more remote and preoccupied.'

Marie looked up at the waiter who had at last arrived to take their order. She ordered a half-bottle of Chardonnay and the plat du jour, as did Corbet. He told the waiter he had enough wine left to accompany his lunch. He knew if he drank any more, he would lose what was left of his ability to concentrate.

'I'm eager to try the stuffed tomatoes,' Corbet couldn't resist adding.

'Oh, they're wonderful, really wonderful.' Marie seemed to welcome the digression from the painful topic of her estrangement from Roger.

'So, that was about how long ago that you noticed this change in Albert?'

'About six months ago, I would say,' Marie said somewhat wistfully. 'Before then he was very busy, but not so preoccupied. When we did spend time together, he was able to concentrate on being with me. It became worse after that.' Her sad expression tugged at Corbet, but he resisted.

'Did his patterns change? Was he out later than usual? Did he not come home?' Corbet needed to ask these painful questions.

'Well, no, that was what was so odd. He didn't really change his schedule at all. He had always spent a lot of time at the Bibliothèque Nationale doing his research and his writing. Roger hadn't been able to get used to writing on a computer and still did all of his writing by hand with a Mont Blanc fountain pen. He said he felt more in control of what he was writing when he could press the pen and ink to the paper rather than finger keys.' These little anecdotes about Albert's work habits seemed to bring Marie closer to him.

'So, he always spent a lot of time working?' Corbet continued.

'Yes, he did. But when he was finished with his daily work, he would come home so exhausted that all he wanted to do was go to bed, to sleep.' She added the last qualifier, and Corbet knew what she meant. He vowed that if he ever had the opportunity to come home to her, he would never only want to go to sleep.

The waiter brought their plats du jour, and Corbet put his fork into the mound of scented rice which tumbled out of the tomatoes. It was marvellous, fresh and aromatic with a light dusting of cheese on top. It was an easy dish to make. He resolved to do more of this type of cooking for himself. After all, it was healthy and rather simple to do. His maternal grandmother used to serve him dishes like this on his sojourns to Nice. Eggplant was another vegetable he enjoyed stuffed.

'He had made a new friend in François de La Roche, the other gentleman who was killed the same night as Roger. I say *was killed*. I assume you're looking at murder in his case?' Marie eyed Corbet, who was still intent on enjoying his stuffed tomatoes.

'Well, we do suspect something of the sort, yes. About this friendship, what do you know about it? How well did they know each other? How much time did they spend together?' Corbet gave his tomatoes a rest.

'It's strange, but I was often jealous of his relationship with de La Roche. He spent a lot of time with him, seemed to really admire him, but never talked much about it. It had even crossed my mind that with the difference in their ages, Roger might be working out some sort of father complex with de La Roche. His father was not very attentive to him, was always busy working on some hot topic or other. He was the famous journalist, Michel Albert.' Marie looked to see if this registered any recognition with Corbet.

'Oh, yes, that fellow. How awful for him.' Corbet didn't like Michel Albert. His caustic style and flip attitude towards the softer side of life, towards man's weaknesses, annoyed him.

'No wonder Roger wanted to work on Proust, a man with such talent and yet so full of human frailties. Not at all a man his father would have admired,' Corbet speculated.

'I guess not. Really, Roger never discussed his work with his father. However, he did spend a lot of time reviewing it with de La Roche. I gather that he had found a very receptive audience in him. He once spoke of having been privileged to read some of the chapters in the memoirs that de La Roche was publishing with Galliante. They had quite an impact on him. He never spoke of the content of the book but often remarked on de La Roche's style and sensibility. Obviously he found it a stark contrast to that of his father.' Marie watched as Corbet put the last precious bite of his tomatoes into his mouth. He savoured the morsel before continuing.

'We often have trouble appreciating our parents and they us.' Corbet stared into the empty booth next to them.

'I've never quite come to terms with my own parents.' Perhaps it was the mellowing effect of the wine and good food that made him wax a bit confessional with Marie. He now felt some desire to tell her why he had never said goodbye to her. She was obviously too polite to ask.

'You know I really missed you after you left Paris.' He continued taking advantage of his surge of courage.

He looked intently at her as she finished the little bit of Chardonnay left in her glass.

'Did you?' She smiled at him. 'Well, I must say I wondered why we never got a chance to say goodbye. I kept hoping to see you at lectures, but you didn't show up before I left.'

'I know.' He wanted to be able to be honest with her, but maybe this wasn't the time or the place. Maybe he should wait until after these cases were over. 'I had some family problems at the time that took all of my attention,' was all he could manage to say by way of explanation.

'At the risk of being very bold, Henri, I must ask you how you came to do this sort of work. I was so surprised when your assistant mentioned your name. At first I thought there was no way it could possibly be the same friend I had at the Sorbonne. But here you are. How did it happen?'

'Well, after you left Paris, I decided to study abroad for a year. I spent one semester at the University of Heidelberg in Germany and another at an institute in Leningrad. You know I've always loved literature. This was my last chance to immerse myself totally in it before dealing with the exigencies of the real world.

'It was while I was studying in Leningrad and reading Dostoyevsky that I became more and more interested in crime and transgression, that weak side of man that won't let him stay within the bounds prescribed for him by society, the side that demands expression against the peace and order of civilisation. For me, Dostoyevsky was a natural spin-off from Stendhal, who glorified his hero and made criminality romantic. To deal with men at the existential edge, I felt might give me more insight into what forms our weaknesses as human beings and into what forges our strengths.' He looked into Marie's eyes. She gazed steadily at him, showing her delight in and surprise at the expression of such a serious side of his character.

'It sounds fascinating,' was all she said.

'Also, as I was growing up, my father had a close friend who was a Chief Inspector with the Paris Police, a Monsieur Mamon. He would often come to dinner, and would talk to me as though he really were interested in my ideas, something my own father didn't do. This was a very educated, cultured and urbane gentleman, really more so than my own father. He became a role model for me.

'When I returned from Leningrad, I spent a lot of time talking with him. He truly loved what he was doing, and it looked more interesting to me than studying law. So, I trained for the job.' Corbet put down his empty glass and looked in the direction of the waiter. He felt as though he could use a strong cup of coffee.

Chapter Seventeen

During the short train ride from Paris to Fontainebleau, Henri Corbet finished reading Balzac's *Le Colonel Chabert*. He was struck by the parallel between the main character and François de La Roche.

Colonel Chabert was taken for dead after the Napoleonic Battle of Eylau and had wandered around for ten years trying to reclaim his identity. Meanwhile, his wife and the society all around him had moved on to a world full of values he didn't understand. Even though he was finally able to position himself so that he could obtain recognition by and a settlement from his wife, Chabert decided in the end to renounce it all and retreat into his inner world. François de La Roche, after having been betrayed by his government, had done that also. His memoirs were his attempt to come to terms with the roots of that resignation.

After putting the book back in his briefcase, Corbet leaned back in his seat and began to think of how his own past had altered his life and about what he had renounced as a result of it. After seeing Marie today, there was no doubt in his mind that he was still very attracted to her. In fact, she had seemed even more appealing in her sorrow and her grief than the carefree young student he had known. He wondered if he dared to let himself hope. Before he could decide yes or no, the train pulled into the station at Fontainebleau.

The Marquis de Courcey had sent a driver and car to pick him up, and they sped away towards Château des Sources.

In the low light of the afternoon the countryside was a welcome change from the bustle of Paris. He wondered why he didn't make a point of getting out of the city more often and resolved to do so.

Château des Sources was situated on the edge of the Fontainebleau forest over a number of underground springs. There was gentle running water everywhere. The château itself had undergone a recent redecoration by the current Marquise de Courcey, who had transformed it into what some called a rather cluttered, English style. Corbet would have said eclectic. The Marquis insisted that they take a walk on the grounds before dinner, and Corbet welcomed the opportunity to stretch his legs and breathe some country air.

The bright afternoon sun of late September joined a fresh breeze to bathe Corbet in glorious light and air. As the Marquis de Courcey proudly showed him the grounds of the château, he pointed out that the countryside provided some of the finest hunting in the region. Indeed it had been for that reason that the early French kings had claimed the territory for hunting and that François I had developed and enlarged the château at Fontainebleau.

'My father has fond memories of hunting here,' Corbet said simply.

'Yes. Your father was a great friend of my father's. I remember his visits when I was a little boy. I'm glad to meet you at last. There was often talk of your father's bringing you down to visit, but it never happened. And now you are here on business and not so pleasant business at that.'

Corbet nodded for him to continue.

'At any rate, you will dine with us tonight. We are having Wilhelm's famous snail soup followed by a fricassée of pheasant with chanterelles. I hope you will like it.' The Marquis continued his long-legged and deliberate walk. He was a very tall, large-boned man with long brown hair which was swept back by the wind as he walked. His gait and appearance spoke of ease and self-possession. Corbet moved quickly to keep up with him.

'It sounds just marvellous. It's been awhile since I've had pheasant.' Corbet knew he had to get on with the task at hand. 'Just what is your memory of life here during the war?' Going directly to the point seemed the easiest way to begin.

'Well, I was quite young, and my memories are vague. But I do remember that the château was always crowded with many different kinds of people, people in brown uniforms who spoke German, our family, the servants, and later the Americans. We had a governess who tried to keep us pretty segregated from the rest of the activity in the château. I remember that my father seemed very preoccupied and often very, very sad. I felt so helpless in the face of that, but would nonetheless try to comfort him.' The Marquis stopped and leaned his arm against a big tree. Corbet was glad for the chance to rest a bit. They sat down under the tree.

'The person who would know more about those times would be Wilhelm. He was a very young German soldier who was stationed here during the war as an assistant to the generals. He stayed on after the war in the American prison camp. He got along so well with everyone that when it was all over he was allowed to remain. His considerable cooking talent also helped persuade my family to keep him on. At any rate, he has become an important member of our staff. You will see why tonight.' The Marquis was picking blades of grass as he spoke.

'Do you think I might speak with him?' Corbet couldn't deny that he wanted to talk to Wilhelm about more than his firsthand knowledge of the war. 'I wouldn't mind going to the kitchen to speak with him, if that's all right with you.' He looked hopefully at the Marquis.

'Of course, you may. He'll be busy preparing dinner, but if he agrees to grant you an audience, I see no reason why you can't talk to him.' Corbet's smile didn't conceal his joy at the prospect. 'There's been a lot of interest in this place lately.' The Marquis looked somewhat inquiringly at Corbet.

'What type of interest are you talking about?' Corbet waited.

'Well, I've had visits from both Thérèse de La Roche and Pierre de La Roche, each on a separate occasion, of course.' The Marquis continued to examine the blades of grass.

'I take it this was before the death of François de La Roche?' Corbet inquired, somewhat surprised at the revelation.

'Oh, yes, of course. They both wanted to know what I knew about François de La Roche and his first wife and son. Apparently he had been writing his memoirs and had mentioned Château des Sources as the place where he had pleaded to no avail with the Germans to save his wife and son. I told them what I've told you about my knowledge. However, I didn't refer them to Wilhelm. I'm not sure exactly why, but my instincts told me to let it rest there, and I did. With you it's different. A man has been killed, and there's a lot more at stake now, to say nothing of the fact that you represent the Paris Police.' The Marquis looked at Corbet with a look of deference, acknowledging the importance of his position. Corbet nodded in reply.

'You say they came separately. Who came first?' Corbet waited.

'It was Thérèse de la Roche who came first. She said she needed more background on her husband's past. She said she was coming on behalf of her son, Pierre. That's why I was quite surprised when about a week later Pierre himself showed up. As I said, I really couldn't tell them anything that they didn't already know.'

'Yes,' was all Corbet said. 'And Thérèse de La Roche...'

'That is one beautiful woman, if you don't mind my saying so.' The Marquis gave Corbet a sidelong glance.

'No, I don't mind, and you're right. She's unforgettable.' Corbet felt at once jealous of the Marquis's response and vindicated for being vulnerable to the charms of Madame de La Roche.

'You know her family used to live nearby, don't you?' The Marquis gazed at Corbet.

'Why, no, I didn't know that. I don't know much about that woman.' Corbet caught himself before he said any more.

'Yes. She was Thérèse d'Aubery, a family with roots in the old noblesse. Her father was a bit of a maverick. He lost most of his money and lands at the time of the war, but was very active in the Resistance. In fact, it cost him his life. He was killed in a raid one night when the Nazis went on an extermination hunt.' The Marquis continued to examine the blades of grass he had picked.

'Did you know Thérèse de La Roche as a child?' Corbet waited eagerly.

'Well, yes and no. I knew of her. I never spent much time in her company. Our families weren't really that close, just more or less neighbours. But I do know that she was as stunning then as she is now. Also, I remember the talk among the locals when she married de La Roche. No one thought for a moment that she had married him for love. He was so much older than she.' The Marquis seemed to get lost in his own thoughts as he stared at the ground.

'Do you think she knew about his role in the Vichy government when she married him?' Corbet pressed on.

'I don't know, but I seriously doubt it. Her father, after all, had been a Resistance hero. It would seem rather odd that she would marry someone like de La Roche if she had known.' The late afternoon sun went behind a cloud, darkening the landscape. The Marquis sat silently for a moment.

'What do you know about a René Simon? I really mean, what do you know about his father?' Corbet pressed on. A little digging into René Simon's background had revealed that indeed he was the son of Charles Simon.

'I know that there was a man named Simon – I'm not sure of his first name, maybe it was Charles or something like that – who was one of the most despised Vichy collaborators. From what I've heard about him, he was a man without scruples who might have been more at home if he could have openly worn a Nazi uniform.' The deep frown on the Marquis's face expressed his intense displeasure at the mention of this man.

'Did you know that his son, René, is a top editor at Galliante?' Corbet probed.

'In some vague way, yes, I guess I did know that. That was a very painful time, and I don't go digging around trying to discover who was what when. What I would find, I'm sure, would be even more distressing than what I know now.' The Marquis seemed almost to be pleading with Corbet to stop the inquiry. He decided to show him some mercy.

'I thank you for your help. My father thanks you too.' Corbet was sure that his father would want to be remembered to the Marquis.

'Well, now we must get you in to see Wilhelm.' The Marquis lifted his tall frame from the ground and stood to his full height. Corbet scrambled up on his knees, then on his full legs, to join him.

Chapter Eighteen

The kitchen of the château was one large, square room with what appeared to be a wall of black stoves on one side, a large wooden table in the middle, and copper pots hanging from everywhere. Corbet's nostrils were treated to the heavenly scent of a game stock which had been cooking for some time.

In front of the wall of black stoves stood a tall hulk of a man dressed in white. He was bending forward and taking the lid off a pot of stock when Corbet entered the room. The Marquis introduced the man in white as Wilhelm Friedheim. Corbet noted that he was a man easily in his sixties, but very well preserved, with rather long grey hair. Judging from the force of his handshake, he was quite strong. He offered Corbet a seat at the wooden table, which he gladly accepted. The Marquis left them to their conversation, saying he was going to rest a bit before dinner.

'You'll forgive me if I keep working?' Wilhelm inquired of Corbet.

'But of course. I know you have to prepare dinner. In fact, I'm very much looking forward to it. Do you mind if I watch you prepare while we chat? I love cooking myself and am always delighted to have an opportunity to watch an artist at work.' Wilhelm nodded.

He came to the table upon which were lying several pheasants. He began to cut them up into pieces – legs and thighs, wings, breasts. Corbet peered into a large bowl of chanterelles waiting for the sauce.

'The Marquis mentioned that you were making a snail soup. I haven't had that since my sojourn in Heidelberg as a young man. The secret to that is the game stock?'

'Absolutely right.' Wilhelm continued to dismember the pheasants with a skill and speed that impressed Corbet. He wanted to keep a close eye on the preparation of the dish so that he might try it at home. Wilhelm left the table and went to the wall of stoves to check the contents of a large copper stockpot. Corbet followed him.

'I hope you don't mind my close observation of your preparations?' The rich, brown scent coming from the copper pot made Corbet swoon. It was the snail soup which had already been prepared and was on the stove on a slow simmer. Corbet began to make mental notes on how to prepare the soup. When Wilhelm returned to his pheasants, Corbet decided it was time to get down to business.

'I understand you've lived at the château a long time, that you stayed on after the war?' He would begin with the easy questions.

'Yes, that's right.' Wilhelm returned to the table and was now in the process of seasoning and coating the pieces of pheasant with flour. Corbet followed and watched as Wilhelm placed the coated pieces on a large platter which he took with him when he again headed towards the wall of black stoves. There were two large copper sauté pans on the stove in which there was a mixture of butter and olive oil. Wilhelm began to place the pieces of pheasant in them to brown. Corbet followed him to the stove.

'I'm very grateful to the Marquis de Courcey. The family has been very good to me. I now consider this my home.' He eyed Corbet steadily as he moved the pieces of pheasant around the pan, seeming to brown them evenly without even watching.

'One could do worse for a home.' Corbet was eager to see what Wilhelm would do next to the little pieces of pheasant. It was just as he had suspected. Wilhelm removed the browned pieces from the pan and put them on a platter. Then he reached for a bottle of Médoc and added some of it to the browned bits left in the pan, taking care to deglaze it.

'You'll let that cook a bit before adding the chanterelles?' The scent of the wine mingling with the juices of the birds was intoxicating. When the glaze had reduced a bit, Wilhelm put the browned pieces of pheasant back in the sauté pans, added the rest of the wine, and turned down the heat under them. He returned to the table and began to prepare the vegetables to accompany the meal.

'It must cook a few minutes before I add the chanterelles.' Wilhelm said the words as though giving a soft order to a subordinate. Corbet sensed that he would get more from this man if he waited for him to take the lead. He was quite certain that even a series of well-placed questions wouldn't yield as much as waiting for Wilhelm to be ready to begin.

'You know I am here about François de La Roche?' This was all Corbet said.

'I know.' Wilhelm continued to prepare the green beans which were to be cooked in a large vat of boiling water. When he finished trimming the beans, and while he waited for the water to boil, he set about chopping a large quantity of shallots. Corbet watched eagerly.

When Wilhelm put the beans in the large vat of boiling water and began to melt a quantity of butter in another large pan, Corbet surmised that he was going to make a shallot butter sauce for the beans. His mouth began to water as he contemplated the combination of that with the fricassée of pheasant and chanterelles.

'He used to come here often when the generals were in charge of the château.' Wilhelm had begun to tell his tale. Corbet waited in silence for the next sentence. 'I noticed him particularly because he didn't seem like all the others. He seemed more gentle, more reluctant, I should say, as though he were going through motions he felt he had to go through, but his heart wasn't in it.' Wilhelm stirred the shallots around in the melted butter.

'I was there when he came to plead with the generals about the deportation of his wife to Poland. It was then that he lost his reluctance and reticence. He seemed genuinely distraught and quite beside himself. He begged them. He pleaded with them. They would not be moved. He was crushed, but continued to plead to save his son. The generals were more lenient with him on that score. His son was allowed to go to England.'

Wilhelm lifted the lid on the cooking pheasant and added the chanterelles.

The aroma from the pot was ambrosia to Corbet's eager nostrils. He felt his mouth begin to water, but he kept quiet for another minute or so while Wilhelm fussed over his creation.

'What do you know about a man named Simon, a Charles Simon?'

'Well, he certainly was different from de La Roche, if that's what you mean. He was known as a local henchman, more violent and hate-filled than the worst of our generals.'

Wilhelm again uncovered the cooking pheasant and stirred his creation. Corbet welcomed the luscious aroma.

'He was responsible for a lot of deaths.' Wilhelm took the large pot containing the beans from the stove and drained them into a colander, running them under cold water to stop the cooking. The beans were a lovely bright green. When they were rinsed and drained, he put them into the large pot containing the melted butter and the slightly sautéed shallots. Corbet stood by eagerly.

'I've had another person make an inquiry of me about de La Roche recently.' Wilhelm held Corbet's eye, inviting him to ask who.

Corbet kept quiet, knowing that Wilhelm would tell him who.

'Yes. I was in a café on the edge of town, a place that I frequent in my off hours. I know everyone there.' He stirred the beans to coat them with the butter.

'I was sitting there having a brandy after a hard day's work here in the kitchen when a rather dishevelled looking man came over to my table and, without asking, sat down and asked if I were Wilhelm Friedheim. I told him that I was, and he began to ask me what I knew about the son of François de La Roche who had gone to England. I told him what I've told you. He didn't seem very satisfied with that, seemed to think I was withholding something. He started to get a little nasty with me, but when I looked him dead in the eye and told him that I knew no more, he stopped. He said he was de La Roche's son by a second marriage, and he wanted to learn more about his half-brother.' Wilhelm checked the pheasants again.

'Was that the end of it?'

'Yes. He left after that, not satisfied but at least not trying to make any trouble.' Wilhelm began to clean up his work-space to prepare to plate the meal.

'Wilhelm, I thank you very much for your help in this matter and for the cooking lesson. It's been a real pleasure, to be equalled, I'm sure, only by eating the bounty of your labours upstairs in the dining-room. I eagerly await that.' Corbet went up the back steps to the main part of the château in anticipation of his feast.

Chapter Nineteen

Inspector Corbet decided to sleep in the next morning. He needed time to begin to absorb the new information. He hoped it would digest as well as his pheasant dinner had. It had been one of his more glorious culinary adventures, and he looked forward to preparing it himself when these murders were solved.

After a leisurely breakfast of fresh orange juice and two of his own home-made croissants, he left 13 rue de Buci for a stroll. He wandered down the little street to where it bisects with the rue de l'Ancienne Comedie. On the corner, he stopped to look in the window of La Librarie du Globe, his favourite Russian bookstore. They had an interesting collection of books in Russian and in French dealing with the history and culture of Russia. He decided to go in and browse around.

Every time he visited this bookstore he resolved to brush up on his Russian. He was just beginning to be able to read it when he stopped his studies. He really wanted to be able to read Tolstoy in the original before he died and vowed to resume his lessons at the *France U.R.S.S.* organisation where he had done some studying after his stay in Leningrad.

He wandered over to the French section of La Librarie and began to browse. A green, leather-bound copy of *La Campagne de Russie 1812* caught his eye. He picked up the luscious book and began to peruse it. He became captivated by the first few pages, the description of the encounter between Alexander I and Napoleon. He was reluctant to put the book back on the shelf and decided to buy it to add to his collection. He would look forward to reading it when this case was over.

He purchased the book, strolled out of the bookstore, and headed down the rue de L'Ancienne Comedie towards the Boulevard St Germain. It was a bright, crisp, late September day, and he headed for the Luxembourg Gardens. He knew he needed to get more exercise, and this would help. Also, sometimes his best ideas came to him when he was walking.

Once in the Luxembourg Gardens, he sat down on a bench and began to read his book on the Russian campaign. The Russian character had always fascinated him, and he was secretly delighted by their show of courage and acumen in outwitting Napoleon, leading him to Moscow only to find it deserted and in flames. They would rather lose their beloved city than be conquered by the French.

He was struck by the lengths to which people would go to avoid capture. He wondered to what lengths the murderer or murderers would go in this case to avoid capture and punishment. He began to feel agitated and got up from the bench to stroll back to the Préfecture, to check with Gilet and Leroux before going to Rouen to talk to Rachel Todd and her boyfriend, whom he now knew to be the first son of François de La Roche.

He decided to lunch at a favourite haunt, Le Vieux Bistro, a lovely restaurant which faces the north wall of Notre Dame. From after the First World War up until the Sixties, the restaurant was called Chez Ma Tante. The woman who ran it then was active in the Resistance and used to shelter English soldiers in her basement while she entertained the Germans upstairs, or so the story went.

Corbet was well known to the staff and was led right away to his favourite table in the corner of the front part of the bar. He knew just what he wanted. He ordered what he usually had when he ate here – beef bourguignon – and today a half-bottle of Badoit rather than wine. He wanted to remain very clear-headed.

The waiter brought the first course of leeks vinaigrette. The cool tartness of the dish soothed Corbet and he began to ponder the case. It seemed that Pierre was turning up everywhere. Simon had a large skeleton in his closet, and God knows what was rattling around in that of Valérie Ribeau, to say nothing of Thérèse de La Roche. He was surrounded by a rather unsavoury bunch of suspects.

Whenever his mind drifted to Thérèse de La Roche, he couldn't help wondering what she didn't tell him. It was certain that she was hiding a lot more than the names of her lovers. He was convinced that what she hadn't told him was probably more important than what she had told him. How to get at it was the problem.

The waiter removed the first course plates and brought him a steaming serving of the beef bourguignon. The heavy, wine-scented aroma wafted its way up to his nostrils. He took his first bite of the little onions along with a lardon bathed in the wine sauce. The flavours played in his mouth like the strings in a Mahler symphony, followed by the brass section of the wine-soaked beef and the potatoes swathed in the sauce, the woodwinds. He often felt that music was so beautiful he could taste it and food so delicious he could hear it. The bourguignon sang. As he mopped up the last of the sauce with the remaining pieces of baguette, he began to consider dessert. He loved the tarte Tatin which the waiter would flambé with Calvados and serve with a large mound of crème fraîche. He ordered it and vowed to eat lightly that evening in Rouen.

Chapter Twenty

The train ride from Paris to Rouen takes one hour. Corbet left late that afternoon. He phoned his friends, Victor and Annette, the owners of a small bookstore in Rouen, to tell them that he would be arriving that evening and would like to see them before going to the monastery to speak to Rachel Todd.

Victor insisted that he should dine with them and spend the night. He would drive him to the monastery in the morning. Corbet agreed, glad for the diversion from his investigation. Somehow he didn't want to spend the night alone tonight. So much had been stirred up by his reunion with Marie. An evening spent in the presence of a happily married couple wouldn't hurt, might renew his faith.

That they were happily married was somewhat of an odd event for both of them. They had met and married late. Before meeting Annette, Victor was about to join an order of monks and had been what he thought was a confirmed homosexual. Annette had been a rather depressed person who had not yet found someone to love. They met, and all of that seemed to change. Victor decided that he wanted to give heterosexuality a chance, and Annette decided that she would let herself love someone. They were married and now expected their first child.

While he enjoyed their company tremendously, Corbet always remained somewhat sceptical about their respective conversions. He never let on, though, and hoped that time would prove him wrong. It seemed to be doing just that.

He had met Victor and Annette during a visit to Illiers/Combray, the home of Proust's Tante Léonie. Victor was a devoté of Proust and had read the whole of *A la recherche du temps perdu* several times. Corbet felt that he would be lucky to read the whole work once in his lifetime. He was impressed by Victor's devotion to books and literature. They spent many hours discussing various writers, and Corbet always left Rouen with a gift from the bookstore.

That evening they dined on raw oysters, salad and fresh bread. The conversation was filled with Victor's curiosity about the Albert case. He had known of Albert's work because of his interest in Proust and had been eagerly awaiting the arrival of his new book. He asked Corbet whether he thought the book would be published anyway, even though not quite complete. Corbet, of course, had no answer for him. He gave what answers he could, but made sure to protect the privacy of the people involved and that of his investigation.

The next morning Victor drove him to the Abbey of Saint Wandrille. The forty-minute journey wound them through the green Normandy countryside sprinkled with salt-and-pepper cows. In what seemed like no time, Victor turned the corner on the country road where the main gate of the monastery beckoned at the end of a short street. The little village church of Saint Saturnin, dating from the tenth century and not really connected with the monastery, nestled down at the left. The monastery gate was of classic eighteenth-century design. As they drove through the grounds, Corbet noted the juxtaposition of centuries, the architecture of ruins from the thirteenth and fourteenth centuries and the remains of the old church from the seventeenth and eighteenth centuries.

Victor introduced him to Frère Sébastien, the affable and courteous hotelier for the St Joseph's Guesthouse. It was located across the street from the monastery and housed lay guests on retreat. Often Victor would come here for two or three days at a time just to read and relax. He was on good terms with Frère Sébastien and assured him that Corbet would be a good guest. Corbet let it go at that for the time being, said goodbye to Victor and mounted the stairs to discover his room. Neither spartan nor luxurious, it was rather small, but not a cell, with a single bed, desk and chair and a window overlooking a back barnyard full of cows grazing on the thickly-grown green.

While settling in his room, Corbet read the little card up over his nightstand which gave the schedule of events at the monastery. It was now only 9.15 a.m., and mass started at 9.30 a.m. He could make it. Even though he was not a practising Catholic – something he wouldn't go into with Frère Sébastien – he enjoyed going to mass, especially a high mass. At the monastery the monks celebrated the mass daily. Corbet entered the church and sat down on one of the spare benches towards the front.

Just ahead of him was a row of young men, novices, who were preparing for their monastic vows. Some of them were very handsome. The church remained silent and was well-lit by many candles. Soon the monks, dressed in black, of all ages – from octogenarians to novices in their early twenties or younger – began to file into the sanctuary singing a heavenly Gregorian chant. Corbet was transported by the beauty of the sound and the smell of the incense being shaken out of the large brass container. He remembered masses he had attended as a child. The Gregorian chant, sung in Latin, of course, acted like a tonic on his frayed nerves, and he felt in danger of forgetting why he was here. He vowed to make a journey back to spend a few days reading and enjoying monastery life once the case was over.

After mass, he returned to his room. He had a bit of time before lunch was served, or so he had been informed by the cook, a village woman who came daily to prepare and serve meals. He took out his rather well-worn copy of *Le Rouge et le noir* and began to read. The pungent and hearty scent of a home-made cassoulet, containing white beans, garlic, onions, tomato sauce, and housing several kinds of meats – goose, pork, lamb, sausage – wafted up to meet him as he prepared to come down to lunch. He descended the stairs, eager to sample this bounty. There would be time enough to get to the business at hand.

Frère Sébastien was the only direct contact that people on retreat would have with the monks. He had come to the dining-room to give the noon prayer and blessing. He informed the guests that it was customary for the noon meal to be taken in silence, but that they could, via the two speakers in either corner of the room, listen to the readings done by the monks in their dining-room.

Corbet savoured the cassoulet, chewed on the brown bread made by the monks and welcomed the tart complement of the gratin of tomatoes and leeks to the reading of *La vie de Louis XVI*. The monks had been reading the biography for some time and had reached the point where Louis XVI was preparing for his execution. The reading monk chanted the rather chilling scenario in a steady, staccato voice.

The reading ended. The guests finished the meal in silence. Corbet noticed that they were as varied as the architecture of the monastery. There was a nun, another woman in her forties, a young man and what appeared to be his mother, and a very old woman with gnarled hands. He felt a pang of guilt about welcoming the chance to enjoy the ambience of the monastery before proceeding with his investigation. He was beginning to wonder where Rachel

Todd and her boyfriend were. He would have to ask Frère Sébastien before long.

After lunch, he retired to the sitting-room in the front of the building. Frère Sébastien came in and joined him. Corbet seized the moment to ask the necessary questions about the whereabouts of Rachel Todd and her companion. Frère Sébastien told him that yes, they had arrived at The Abbey of Saint Wandrille yesterday, but had left very early that morning for a day trip to Jumièges, a neighbouring village, where there were wonderful ruins of an eleventh century abbey which, the good father was happy to point out, had been consecrated in 1067 by the archbishop of Rouen in the presence of William the Conqueror. The gentleman was interested in church architecture and history and seemed quite excited about the prospect of visiting the site. The lady, Frère Sébastien thought, seemed a bit preoccupied. Otherwise, they were a perfectly lovely couple. Engaged to be married, he thought. Of course, they had separate rooms as did everyone who visited the monastery, he was quick to add. They would be back for dinner.

Reassured, Corbet decided to have a quiet read and then have tea at the little Crêperie/Salon de Thé across from the village church. He had noticed it coming in this morning. Often in these little, out-of-the way tea shops one could sample some rather sumptuous pastries. After his read, having left Julien Sorel at the beginning of his apprenticeship at the house of the Marquis de La Mole, he left the guesthouse for a walk before his tea.

The countryside around the monastery was lovely enough to convert the most anti-bucolic being to an appreciation of its beauty. He particularly enjoyed a conversation he had with some goats. They seemed to take great delight in 'baaing' at him. Later when he asked the young waitress at the tea shop if their vocalisations meant that he had frightened them, she informed him that that was their way of saying *'Bienvenue'*.

He drank his tea – good hot English tea – and ate some fresh-baked madeleines. The baker had been generous with the lemon peel, and they were delicately scented with it. He allowed his mind to wander back to his encounter with Marie. On the whole, he was really delighted to have her in his life again, even if it had to happen under these gruesome circumstances. He looked forward to having the opportunity to be of some comfort to her. If he could solve these murders, he was sure he would put her mind at ease. He left the tea shop, leaving the serving girl a generous tip.

Back in his room, he resumed his reading and then undressed for a late afternoon nap before supper. He got into bed and was drifting off when he heard heavy footsteps coming down the hall. The loud knock at his door rattled his composure. When he asked who it was, Frère Sébastien responded in a quiet but rather urgent voice that he needed to speak to him right away.

Corbet dressed, descended the stairs and entered the front sitting-room. Frère Sébastien was waiting for him along with a local police officer. The officer introduced himself and told Corbet that there was a death that had to be investigated. A young man had just died in the Salon de Thé across the street. The body was being taken to Rouen to determine the cause of death. He was drinking tea and had been accompanied by a young lady. She was now in her room at the monastery in a very shaken condition.

Corbet's head began to swim. How fast this had all happened! He told the officer that he himself had just left the tea salon not more than an hour ago. They must have come in just after he left. He liked the young local officer who seemed eager to do his job and very inclined to be helpful. Corbet quickly updated him about his reason for being at the monastery in the first place. He kept casting an eye towards Frère Sébastien to reassure him that in spite of his real mission he had gotten some spiritual benefit from his brief stay at the Abbey of St Wandrille.

The good father seemed to understand and was very concerned about the lady's state of mind. Would Corbet talk to her? Of course he would. He needed to do that anyway, but this really served to complicate matters. The young officer informed him that the crime scene had been secured, and Corbet accompanied him back there.

The serving girl was very shaken and told them with a broken and trembling voice what she had observed. The couple had come into the restaurant and ordered tea. They were the only customers in the restaurant at the time. The man was in a good humour and very outgoing, the woman not so much.

They ordered tea and madeleines, the same thing the Inspector had ordered just an hour before. Corbet felt a chill when he realised that he might have been the victim. She prepared the tea and served them. Shortly thereafter, the gentleman seemed to choke, and the lady tried to get him to drink some water, but to no avail. He dropped to the ground rather quickly. The serving girl called the police immediately. That was all she could tell them.

The young officer told Corbet that the cups and dishes were being taken to the lab for tests. Corbet asked the young woman if she had left the teapot or the cups unattended at any time during the preparation of the tea. She thought a moment and then told him that she had received a phone call while she was preparing their order. She had in fact left the back room of the kitchen for just a few moments to come to the counter to speak with her father, who had telephoned and asked her to pick up some medicine for her mother on the way home. The call had taken not much more than a minute, maybe two at the most. She said she hadn't noticed anything strange, and then she stopped short. Yes, she had noticed that the top had been removed from the teapot. She thought she had left it with the top on it while she boiled the water. She remembered questioning herself about this, but didn't make too much of it.

The tea was served to both the gentleman and the lady. It came out of the same pot, but only one person died. Apparently the woman had not drunk hers yet and was soon distracted by the gentleman's difficulties. Corbet thanked the serving girl and told the local officer he would be in touch with him soon. He headed back to the monastery to talk to Rachel Todd.

Chapter Twenty-One

Inspector Corbet found Rachel Todd waiting for him in the front sitting-room. He observed a slight woman of medium height, in her early thirties, with shining auburn hair, walking rather aimlessly around the room. She seemed at once stunned and agitated. Corbet introduced himself and asked her to sit down.

'It's been just awful for me. Since my arrival in Paris, I've felt pursued by some unspeakable evil. And now Gerard is dead. It's all so utterly unbelievable.'

Corbet nodded his head. She seemed grateful for the chance to talk to someone who appeared to want to listen to her.

'How soon after your arrival did you begin to notice this sense of strangeness?'

'Oh, it really happened on the train ride up from Bordeaux. I had been visiting with some friends down there and was on my way up to Paris to get installed in my living quarters for the semester at Bryn Mawr – I'm a graduate student there – when a man died on the train near Poitiers.'

'Yes. That was François de La Roche,' Corbet added.

'And then I later found out that he was the father of the man from whom I was renting my studio apartment.

'Also, the very evening of my arrival in Paris, after Pierre de La Roche had settled me into my studio, I heard an ambulance and a lot of noise outside in the street, and they carted someone off from a restaurant next door. I later learned that that was Roger Albert, a friend of my boy-friend, Gerard. It's all been so unbelievably eerie.'

The release of being able to give vent to all of the ten-sion showed itself when tears began to run down Rachel's cheeks. She sobbed rather quietly. Corbet took her hand, hoping to steady her for the more painful and difficult questions to come.

She nodded her appreciation, took some strength from the support and went on.

'When we came down here for the long weekend, I had hoped that we would find some peace. Gerard was quite upset over the news of Albert's death. He had become good friends with him when Albert was a guest lecturer at Oxford a few years back. However, he was determined to get on with his research on the French and English Catho-lic churches. We thought this little trip to the Abbey of Saint Wandrille would help us both.' She paused, grew silent and seemed to stare at a spot on the rug. Corbet waited for her to resume.

'I can't believe this has happened.' She fell silent again. Her mind seemed to be struggling to get used to an awful and unacceptable idea. 'I can't believe he's…'

She stopped short of saying the word. Corbet looked at her in silence. Tears streamed down her cheeks again. A strong sense of compassion filled Corbet's heart. He could identify with the loss of a valued loved one.

'Perhaps we had better wait until tomorrow to finish this,' he offered.

'No, I really want to do it now while it's all fresh in my mind.' Rachel seemed to regain some strength.

Corbet didn't argue with her.

'When did you meet Gerard Goode?' he asked.

'I met him when I was in London this summer. He was the tutor of one of my friends who was studying at Oxford, a tutor in French history. The attraction was immediate. I knew I had met someone very special. I was still getting used to the idea that I was going to have someone…' She trailed off again. Corbet began to wonder whether he was up to watching her struggle with her pain. He decided that if she could endure it so could he. He waited.

'Yes, go on,' he said when he felt she could do it.

She seemed to welcome the invitation. 'He had come over to visit me and help me get settled in Paris. Oxford doesn't start until October, so he had some time. In spite of this eerie cloud that seemed to hang over us, I was very happy with him. He was truly special.' She seemed now to take comfort from remembering the positive things about her dead companion.

'Tell me more about Goode's relationship with Albert.' Corbet decided to move ahead.

'Well, as I said, they had met when Albert was lecturing on Proust at Oxford. Gerard had an interest in French literature and got to know him then. They had kept in contact.

'In fact, recently Albert had visited him at Oxford and told him that he thought he had met someone in Paris who might be very important to him. Gerard had grown up in England with adoptive parents, but he had always been told that his parents were French, that he had been born in Paris. He never knew who they were, just that they had run upon some misfortunes, and he was given up for adoption. Albert, of course, knew this and had become acquainted with a man in Paris whom he thought might be Gerard's father.

'Gerard was ecstatic at the possibility at long last of meeting his father. Albert didn't tell him who it was, but did indicate that when Gerard arrived in Paris this fall he would arrange a meeting.

'I wasn't aware of all of this until our trip down here when Gerard told me all about it after he had learned of

Albert's death. He was, of course, very disturbed to have lost such a friend, but he was also very disappointed that he would never have the opportunity to meet the man Albert had told him about. It was just this morning that he finally told me it was de La Roche.'

Corbet sat in silent wonder. Now the rope was twisting together. De La Roche and Gerard were linked to Albert by friendship and to each other by blood. Who would want them all dead?

'How did you come to rent the de La Roche studio?' Corbet needed to probe further and get her version of the events.

'Well, a friend of mine in London knew some people who had attended Bryn Mawr's Paris program, and they knew Pierre or knew of Pierre. He seems to be interested in foreign students and knows quite a few of them. They said he was visiting London, and they introduced me to him. He took a real interest in helping me find lodging. I understand that his family has always rented the studio to foreign students. He's really an odd duck, though.'

Corbet couldn't have agreed more, but merely inquired, 'So, he made the contact with you for the rental?'

'Well, no, not exactly. He recommended me to a woman at school named Valérie Ribeau. She's in charge of housing the students in the Bryn Mawr program. She contacted me and told me that there was a one-room studio available with a bath and a small kitchen. It sounded perfect for me, and I jumped at the chance to have it. I didn't want to live with a family and couldn't afford a larger apartment in Paris.

'Actually, it's quite fine, except I haven't really been able to enjoy being in it with all of this going on.' She lapsed again into silence, as though trying to recall what it was like before this whirlpool of events.

'You say Gerard was looking forward to meeting this man whom Albert thought might be his father. Had Albert told him why he had been taken from his father in the first place?' Corbet wanted to explore all these connections.

'Well, yes. He had told him that his father had been an official in the Vichy government during the Second World War and that his mother, who had been of Jewish origin, had been taken off. Because he was just a child, and a male child at that, and connected the way he was, de La Roche had had the chance to have him deported to England in order to avoid the fate of his mother.

'Gerard was adopted by a very well-established English family. His father had always sent anonymous support to them, although they really didn't need it. They were quite well off themselves. Gerard was only told that his family had been unable to keep him and had seen to it that he had been well taken care of by the Goodes. He really never knew any more than that until about six months ago when Albert contacted him and told him he might have some information on the whereabouts of his father. He was very excited at the prospect of meeting his father and learning more about his origins.'

Rachel's spirits seemed to sink again after her last statement. She seemed to keep running into the fact that now Gerard would not be able to do anything he had wanted to do or that she had hoped that they might do together. She sat in silent sadness.

Corbet took her hand again as much to help himself as her. She seemed glad of the support, sighed and said she wanted to continue.

'So, he knew nothing about de La Roche or his second family, his wife and Pierre?' Corbet inquired.

'No, not until he came here to visit me. When he met with Albert the very day that Albert died, he told him. It wasn't until then that Gerard became aware of the fact that de La Roche was the man whom Albert had thought was his father.'

'Well, why didn't he come to the police about this?'
Corbet had to ask.

'When Gerard had heard of Albert's death, as well as that
of de La Roche, he had thought of going to the police but
had decided to wait until after our weekend down here to
gather himself for the prospect of what he might find out.

'Also, I must confess that I was really spooked by all of
the apparent coincidences and needed some time myself to
deal with it all. We were going to address it when we got
back to Paris, really.' Corbet believed her.

'Well, that will be all for now. I would take you back
with me to Paris this evening, but I think you should rest
and come tomorrow. I'll make arrangements with the
school to have someone come down to accompany you
back.' It was the least he could do. Rachel nodded gratefully
and seemed glad for the opportunity to escape her pain with
a few hours of sleep.

As she left to head upstairs to her room, Corbet was
struck by the smell of braised beef, onions and carrots
coming from the kitchen. Maybe he would have time to
stay for supper before going back to Paris.

After having relished the homey dish provided to the
guests at St Joseph's, Corbet took a cab to the train station
in Rouen and got the 9 p.m. train for Paris. He settled into
his seat and began to digest the day's events along with his
evening meal. Yet another murder, and now no doubt that
they were all connected. He would have to move fast when
he got back to Paris.

A man came by selling candy and newspapers. Corbet
realised that he had not read a paper in a while and bought
one. On the second page there was a small notice at the
bottom indicating that there had been an arrest in that old
murder case in Bordeaux. No names were given. The
police simply had made an arrest. Corbet felt somewhat
reassured by this news. At least the police eventually found

their culprit. Maybe he would find his, too. But what if it took that long? Oh, not to torture himself with those negative thoughts. He suddenly realised how tired he was and dozed the rest of the way back to Paris. Often he found he was able to make many of the subtle connections in a case in his sleep, so to speak, calling upon his deeper, less conscious powers, those that Dostoyevsky liked to call deep penetration.

Chapter Twenty-Two

At 11 p.m. Inspector Corbet arrived home and was greeted by an angry, lonely and anxious Michelet, who rubbed around his legs and eyed him suspiciously and longingly. Corbet reached down and picked him up, hugging him tightly and telling him that he had missed him very much. Michelet softened and received the affection.

'Didn't Madame Lissard treat you well?' he asked, knowing full well that Laura Lissard was a very responsible cat-tender whom he had used for many years. Michelet buried his head in Corbet's shoulder as if to say, 'All right, but not as well as you.' Corbet squeezed him, kissed his neck and put him down again on the floor. Fences were definitely mending.

The apartment seemed strange, an atmosphere of worldly sophistication compared to the spare quarters of the monastery. He settled into bed with his new book on the Russian campaign, hoping it would help him unwind and fall asleep. Michelet snuggled next to him, purring in forgiveness.

He had just fallen asleep with the book on his chest and the light still on when the phone startled him out of his repose. It was Gilet checking to see if he had gotten back all right and what he had found out. Oh, yes, and to let him know that the Rouen police had concluded that Goode's death was the result of cyanide poisoning, and there were no fingerprints found at the scene.

Well, here he had all three murders with the same *modus operandi*, poison in tea, being drunk with madeleines. Clearly, they were all connected. Were they all done by the same person? Corbet agreed to meet Gilet and Leroux first thing in the morning at the Quai des Orfèvres. He fell back into a troubled but deep sleep.

The next morning he went into his office and settled into his chair to drink his coffee and help himself to one of his chocolates. The weight of the case, the impact of Thérèse de La Roche, the reunion with Marie, the murder at the monastery, all had begun to take a toll on him. But he could not falter now. He needed to keep going. He had to get to the bottom of this.

His attention was suddenly grabbed by the noise of the collision of two bodies in his office doorway. Gilet's slender body had collided with the burly musculature of Leroux's as they both tried to enter Corbet's office at once. They both laughed, and Gilet backed away to let his heftier counterpart pass through.

When they were both in front of Corbet's desk, they began to talk at the same time. Corbet put his hand up to signal the need for some restraint and continued to chew on his chocolate. Between the two of them, they finally were able to communicate to Corbet that the Bordeaux police had phoned and said that they had a man down there who had confessed to one of the murders, one of the madeleine murders.

'Which one?' Corbet demanded somewhat irritably.

'De La Roche. He says he didn't do the Albert murder, and he couldn't have done the Goode murder since he was in Bordeaux being arrested for an old crime, the murder of a young, pregnant woman which had been on the books for some time.' Gilet was so full of the news that his delivery was anything but smooth.

'Go on.' Corbet needed more information. Gilet and Leroux alternately proceeded to fill his ears with the fact that this man, Jules Flagon, said that he had been black-mailed into murdering de La Roche by someone who knew of his past wrongdoing with the young woman. Once he had been arrested for the first crime, he saw no need to keep the other a secret. The Bordeaux police were still having trouble getting the name of the blackmailer out of him, but they were going to keep working on him. Also, they had found a container which they thought had contained the cyanide. On it were the fingerprints of Flagon and a faint set of prints belonging to someone else.

'All right. Let's say that he did really kill de La Roche. But who killed Albert and Goode? We still don't have an answer to that. They were killed in pretty much the same way.' Corbet was chewing on the end of a pencil and leaving bite marks.

'The police are withholding Flagon's identity from the press because they don't want to scare off the blackmailer,' Gilet added impulsively.

'Yes, yes, but of course they are. But we've got no prints from the silver pillbox or from any of the cups or objects at the crime scenes. That's what makes these prints so important. I want you to make sure we have sets of prints from all the suspects: Thérèse de La Roche, Valérie Ribeau, Simon, and Pierre.' Corbet kept wondering why Flagon, the very Flagon who had been hired help at the de La Roche château for so many years, didn't want to reveal the identity of his blackmailer. He didn't like the uncomfortable feeling he was getting when he thought of Thérèse de La Roche, whom he intended to contact that very morning for another interview.

He cleared Gilet and Leroux out of his office and dialled the château at Bordeaux. He was told by the butler that Madame de La Roche had left last night for Paris. He dialled the Paris number, and that voice answered the phone. Corbet was not unaffected by it but stuck to his mission.

'I've called to inquire whether we might meet again for some more conversation.' This seemed gentle enough.

'I also need to see Pierre,' he added somewhat as an afterthought.

'Well, Pierre's not here. He has gone to Rouen, or I should say to outside of Rouen to escort Rachel Todd back to Paris. He said Valérie called this morning and asked that he do that, and, of course, he said he would.' Her voice was soft and hypnotic.

'However, you can see me tomorrow. In fact, I'm having a gathering here at the apartment, sort of a memorial service for François. His funeral will be over then, and we will all gather back here for some conversation and refreshments. I would really like you to come.' The hypnosis continued. 'Will you?'

'Of course I will. But I had rather hoped that I might interview you alone before that.' Corbet tried to be as considerate as possible under the circumstances.

'Well, it must be after, then. I have so much to do to get ready for all of this. I know you understand.' Corbet did. He agreed to come to the Paris apartment at 2 p.m. the next afternoon for the gathering to honour François de La Roche.

He replaced the receiver and continued to chew on the now very dented pencil. Pierre had gone to Rouen to get Rachel Todd. That made him very uneasy. Valérie Ribeau had not indicated that she intended to send him. She had merely said that she would send someone to accompany her back. He should have specifically requested that it be someone from the school. At the very best, it would be an uncomfortable journey for Rachel, and it could be more than uncomfortable.

He reached for the receiver and asked Gilet to go down to Rouen and see if he could connect up with Pierre and Rachel, tail them loosely so as not to alarm anyone. First he would telephone the monastery to see if Rachel had left yet. She had, he was told by Frère Sébastien. They had just hired a car to drive them to Rouen. They would probably take the 10 a.m. train for Paris. He called Gilet back and told him to get down to the train station and wait to follow them when they arrived back in Paris.

Meanwhile, he called the Rouen police and asked that someone be put on the 10 a.m. train to tail Pierre. He gave a description of him and Rachel. The officer said he would see to it right away. Somewhat relieved, Corbet leaned back in his chair and began to think about re-encountering Thérèse de La Roche.

Chapter Twenty-Three

Jacqueline Champigneulle occupied an amazing studio apartment with a set of very large windows that looked directly into the stained glass of a church across the lane. The walls were covered with a large-patterned, red floral tapestry-like material with a beige background. A long empire sofa in red almost took up one wall. Opposite the windows, on the other side of the room, were two small doorways, one leading to a compact, well-equipped kitchen and the other to a large bathroom with a huge claw-foot tub in the centre of the room. If surroundings reflect their occupants, this was one interesting woman, Corbet was certain of that.

He had decided to go and interview Jacqueline in an effort to continue to knit up all the loose ends of the case. She told him she could give him an hour and no more. He said that would be fine. She motioned for him to be seated on the empire sofa while she herself took a large, high-backed chair near the window. She was dressed in black, simple and chic. Her ivory skin and dark brown hair swept back in a French twist echoed the elegant simplicity of her costume and complemented the bold and dramatic backdrop of the apartment. Corbet was fascinated.

'You're a friend of René Simon, I take it?' Corbet began his inquiry as gently as possible.

'Well, you could say that, yes.' She smiled a Mona Lisa and lowered her eyelids, revealing long thick lashes. Corbet was charmed and intrigued.

'I must tell you I've already spoken with M. Simon, who has revealed the nature of your relationship. You can rely on my discretion.' He looked her straight in the eyes and smiled. She returned a smile of understanding and acknowledgement.

'The night of the de La Roche and Albert murders, last Saturday night between 8 and 10.30 p.m., were you having dinner with René Simon?'

'As a matter of fact, I was.' She smiled that mysterious smile again. 'Why do you ask? Do you think that René had something to do with the murders?' She raised her well-shaped eyebrows and looked at him.

'That's what I'm trying to find out. I have to check on the whereabouts of everyone who could possibly have had a motive to kill either or both of those men.' Corbet sighed and continued. 'Simon was the editor for both men, who were each about to publish a somewhat controversial book, and I need to explore those connections.'

'Connections.' Jacqueline fixed on the word and fell somewhat numbly silent. She continued to look at Corbet as though trying to make up her mind about something. Corbet gave her the room he felt she needed. There was more silence.

Finally she spoke.

'Well, exactly what did René tell you about his relationship with me?' She asked in a firm manner.

'That you were seeing one another without the knowledge of your husband, that I should respect that with discretion and that he had met you through Thérèse de La Roche with whom he used to be involved. That's about it.'

'How interesting. He didn't tell you that he was still wildly obsessed with Thérèse, did he?' Her eyes challenged him.

'Well, no, he didn't. He implied that that was a thing of the past and that he was rather actively involved with you, as a matter of fact.'

'As a matter of fact. Well, he does see me now and again, and I know that he enjoys my company, as I do his, in a manner of passing the time, so to speak. But I really must tell you this isn't what you would strictly call a love affair. He misled you about that. It's a liaison, an arrangement convenient to both parties.' She continued to gaze directly into Corbet's eyes.

'I see.' He contemplated this new wrinkle. 'You mean he's really still very involved with Thérèse de La Roche?'

There was that name again, that woman, that Helen of Troy who seemed to capture the attention of men and hold them in her spell without mercy. Well, he could understand if Simon had been granted some favours by Thérèse and if she had backed off, how he could still be tempted to hang around her like a dog begging for food. It would certainly have happened to him, too, if he had been given the opportunity of a closer encounter with her. He could understand that.

'Simon is a very complicated man, an interesting man.' She continued. 'He has a slick and cool exterior, but he's really quite passionate underneath that façade. Oh, not about me, I tell you, but about what he likes and doesn't like, what he wants. He's very tenacious. I think that Thérèse's new affair with that other author, the man who was writing on Proust...'

'Albert?' Corbet interrupted her and could not hide his surprise at this revelation.

'Yes. I think that's his name. Roger Albert. He was a friend of François's. Simon was impressed with him. Thought he had a wonderful book about to be published. He was rarely jealous of anybody, but he was mad with jealousy over Albert's relationship with Thérèse and over

Albert himself for his unadulterated talent. Of all of
Thérèse's liaisons, this had threatened him the most. He
thought this man might be able to go to places with her that
he himself was unable to go. He was obsessed with this.

'Also, you must realise that when someone functions as
an editor, however good he may be in that capacity, it's still
different from being the author, the one who creates the
work. I think Simon always wished that his talent were
more original and not limited to the revision of the fruits of
the gifts of others.'

She paused and took out a cigarette, looking at Corbet,
waiting for him to light it. He fumbled with a box of
matches on the table in front of the sofa and got up to do
the honours. She inhaled deeply and looked at him.

'I didn't mean to talk so much. In fact, I feel a bit like a
traitor. René warned me that you were coming to talk to
me. He asked me not to say too much, but only to corroborate his story. Maybe I'm releasing my anger and pent-up
frustration by telling you more. I'm sure that René would
not be happy if he knew I had told you all of this. He
merely expected me to corroborate his alibi. Well, I've done
that, and I don't think I've hurt him. I hope not. But I really
think you should know.' She was drawing deeply on her
cigarette as though contemplating something further.
Corbet allowed the silence. Finally she spoke.

'There's something else I think you should know.' She
looked up at Corbet.

'Yes.' He looked back at her and waited.

'Perhaps because of his elegant good looks, I'm not sure
exactly why, but René also attracted many homosexual
men. He used to say that if he entered a crowed room and
there was one gay man present, he would find him and
begin to pester him. Often when we were together these
men would try to flirt with him. He was polite and always
firmly refused their attentions. Most of the time that first

refusal was enough. They would simply depart and look for other prey.

'However, this was not the case with that son of François de La Roche, Pierre. He was very drawn to René and used to haunt him in a way that was not only annoying but also frightening. He always seemed a little bit out of control. René would often meet with François at their Paris apartment, and Pierre made it a point to be lurking around somewhere in the background. He would ask René to lunch. He would call him at the office on all sorts of wild pretexts. Had he left his gloves at the apartment? Did he manage to get all of the manuscript his father had given him? Did he leave a scarf in the hallway? Would he please have a drink with him – he had a book he wanted to write and would like to talk to him about it. He was a terrible pest.' She paused to catch her breath and put out her cigarette.

'Go on,' Corbet urged, eager to hear more about this new connection.

'Well, most of the time René was able to field his attention without having to come out and insult him or risk damaging his relationship with his father. However, it was getting to the point where a confrontation was inevitable, where René would have to tell him firmly to stay away and quit haunting him or he would go to his father. He didn't want to have to do that. He was having enough problems with François over the manuscript. He didn't need more. That's about it. Now you have it.' She crossed her legs, sighed and eyed Corbet as he shifted his solid form on the sofa.

'Was there any connection' – there was that word again – 'that you know of between Albert and Pierre?' Corbet waited for her answer.

'Well, now that you mention it, I believe that René also told me that Albert had mentioned that Pierre was pestering him. It seems that he was also quite attracted to Albert and had let him know it.'

'What did Pierre think of the relationship between Albert and de La Roche, the sort of father-son type relationship?' Corbet again shifted his position on the sofa and waited for her answer.

'I don't know Pierre. I only know of him through my connection with René. I do believe that René mentioned that Pierre was quite resentful of this relationship. Apparently François had all but ignored him while he was growing up. At least that's what Thérèse had told René.'

'Well, I'm sure he was not pleased to see his father showering such paternal attention on another man.' Corbet decided to dive for the big fish. 'Did Pierre know about Albert's relationship with Thérèse?' He waited.

'I'm not sure. I don't think he did. I know that Pierre was very close with his mother, and I'm sure that would not have set too well. In fact, I'm sure if he had known, he would have told François in order to ruin their relationship. So, based on that, I'm pretty sure he didn't know of it.'

'I wonder.' Corbet sat in silence and stared into thin air. Jacqueline waited. She reached for another cigarette. Corbet lit it in silence, running over in his mind all of the new data he had collected, sorting it to make sure that each bit went into its proper place.

'Inspector, I would appreciate it if you would not tell René that I've told you all of this. Of course, if you have to, I'll understand, but if there is any way you can avoid it, please try to do it for my sake.' Jacqueline held her cigarette in the air and waited for his reply. Corbet looked up and nodded at her in the affirmative.

'Well, I thank you, Madame Champigneulle. You've been helpful, very helpful.' Corbet still seemed distracted as he got up from the sofa and held his hand out to say goodbye to Jacqueline.

'My pleasure.' Jacqueline took his hand in farewell and began to escort him to the door. Once out in the street, Corbet's head began to clear a little. He had to get back to the Préfecture to see if Gilet had anything to report on the arrival of Rachel and Pierre in Paris.

And then there was Marie. Poor Marie. Should he tell her about Albert? Was there any way he could avoid doing that? He would ask her to dinner, maybe at La Tour d'Argent. The restaurant had been getting some bad press lately, but he remembered that they had the most wonderful duck. He wouldn't let hearsay from tourists colour his opinion. They actually numbered the ducks they prepared and gave you a card with your duck's number on it. A bit barbaric perhaps, but interesting. And the view was not to be believed. Yes, he would do that. If he had to tell her, this would be a better place to do it than in a café.

Chapter Twenty-Four

Corbet was still reeling from the disclosure of Thérèse de La Roche's involvement with Albert when he headed at a good clip down the Boulevard St Michel towards the Cluny Museum, France's national museum of the Middle Ages. Often when he was in the eye of some contemporary storm, he found it soothing to go to the Cluny Museum and immerse himself in the past, in an age in many ways very different from his own.

He headed right for the room displaying the tapestry of the Lady and the Unicorn. It was a series of several panels depicting the five senses. In the presence of these objects, which in themselves were such a sensual delight with the blue and red, gold and silver of the threads, Corbet began to think about renunciation. The vibrant colours reached out to him, pulling his gaze towards them, and he surrendered himself to them. They seemed to whisper a deeper message about renunciation, something along the lines of 'it is by giving up that we get'. He sat there in the room, surrounded by the splendour of the tapestries, giving up for the moment his struggle with the case at hand, renouncing it and letting his mind go blank.

After several minutes of meditation and contemplation of the tapestries, he moved to another room in the museum. In it were a number of fourteenth- and fifteenth-century choir-stall benches with very amusing carvings on the misericords on the undersides of the seats, showing the vital sense of humour of the woodcarver.

The importance of the pictorial in an age where not many people read always urged Corbet to pretend that he couldn't read and that he had to get his information from the pictures and works of art that graced his life.

He wandered into another room and found himself staring at a whole group of statues of the Madonna and child. There were probably a dozen or so in a group, with all manner of Madonna – smiling, sad, contemplative – and all manner of infant – sleeping, smiling, sombre. He stood there for some time just staring, pondering these depictions of this most central of human relationships. The power of a mother over her child was awesome, a tremendous force for good or evil.

He thought of the hypnotic magnetism of Thérèse de La Roche and how that must have affected the little Pierre, coming into a world where his natural father really wanted nothing to do with him. How vulnerable that made him to his mother, a mother who had her own axe to grind with his father. Strange how she had not mentioned her aristocratic background and yet Pierre seemed obsessed with it.

A woman like Thérèse, once wounded, he imagined would be a formidable foe, capable of almost anything. François de La Roche was dead, murdered by cyanide in tea. Roger Albert was dead, murdered by cyanide in tea. And now Gerard Goode was dead, murdered by cyanide in tea. Corbet glanced up into the eyes of a particularly beneficent Madonna who seemed to bid him continue. The choice of poison as a means of killing was now beginning to make sense. It was not a solution that was pleasant for Corbet to envision.

He left the group of Madonna and child statues and continued to wander in the museum. Whenever he contemplated the art and architecture of the Middle Ages he was always awe-struck at how the urge for redemption had motivated men to build such edifices as Notre Dame and

Chartres cathedrals. In many ways life was harder then, but simpler. You sacrificed this life for the reward in the next. No effort was too great for that. Redemption seemed to be a basic human need with a great power to push men onward.

Was it that need for redemption that had taken hold of de La Roche and forced him to confront his past no matter what the cost, indeed, at the cost of his life? It appeared to be so. For de La Roche it was the publishing of the memoirs that would redeem him. For Simon it was getting the love of a particular woman that he thought would redeem him. For Pierre it was the struggle to get back to an original state with his mother where he could have her to himself. And, yes, for him maybe it was reuniting with Marie.

Chapter Twenty-Five

The Angelina tea room was crowded as usual. Corbet was seated at a table near the window and decided to wait for Rachel Todd before ordering. He looked up to see her enter the door. She looked pale and a bit distracted. When she joined him at the table, she seemed relieved to see a sympathetic and familiar face.

'The agony continues.' She sat down, and Corbet noticed that her hair was a bit dishevelled and that she was not dressed quite warmly enough for the breezy day it was out there.

'Tell me what happened to you. Pierre accompanied you from Rouen to Paris?' he asked, knowing the answer.

'Yes, he did. It was a very curious ride. I know he has always been odd, but...' She trailed off and stared into space. Corbet waited a bit.

'Curious in what way, Mademoiselle Todd?' He pulled her back from her reverie.

'He was extremely solicitous of me. Kept looking at me with very sad eyes and asking me if there was anything he could do. Said he was terribly sorry about Gerard. I just told him that I needed to be quiet, but he kept fussing over me. Kept asking me if I wanted some tea. When the vendor came down the aisle, he took it upon himself to order me a tea, even though I told him I didn't want it. Also, he was twisting a napkin, a linen napkin with a monogram on it, the entire way. He would sometimes use it to wipe the sweat from his brow. He was sweating, even though it was cool in the train.' She paused to catch her breath.

The waitress came over to take their orders. Corbet ordered his favourite crème de marron Chantilly. He needed something soothing at this point. Rachel ordered tea and a strawberry tart.

'Go on,' Corbet urged her to continue.

'Sometimes he would try to take my hand in his in what seemed to be an attempt to offer me sympathy.' She paused to make room for the waitress's delivery of the tart. Corbet plunged his spoon into his chestnut purée and savoured its sweet comfort.

'Did he give you any trouble when you got back to Paris? Did he escort you home from the train station?' He continued to eat his delight.

'Oh, yes. He ordered a cab at the train station. I came directly back to the studio, and he left me at the door. I must confess that I was glad to be back.' She took a bite of her tart and a sip of tea.

'Well, don't worry about tonight and the time thereafter. We have someone guarding your studio. You'll be safe.'

'Thank you.' Rachel lowered her eyes. She seemed to take comfort from Corbet's presence and his reassurances. 'I can't wait until this is all over with. I don't know if I'll ever recover enough concentration to finish my program of study here. I may have to take a break and come back when I've had time to get over all of this.' She looked at Corbet.

'Yes, I can see that. It might be easier if you were not in a foreign country, if you had some old friends around.' His heart went out to her, but he had to move on. 'The night you came from Bordeaux to Paris on the train, the night that de La Roche died, what time did you get into Paris?'

'Must have been around – I was so rattled from the events on the train that I don't remember noticing the time, but it must have been around nine-thirty or so.'

'You went directly to the rue du Mt. Thabor?'

'Yes, I took a taxi from the Gare d'Austerlitz.' Rachel stiffened a bit as she continued. 'Pierre met me at the door and showed me my studio. He also offered me some tea in his parents' apartment.'

'Did you notice anything unusual about him at that time? What was his mood, his frame of mind?' Corbet probed.

'Not really anything other than that he seemed like an odd person to begin with, unkempt, somewhat distracted, very talkative.' She seemed to search her memory for more details.

'How long were you with him then?'

'Oh, maybe about half an hour, while he gave me tea and talked to me about former students who had lived in the studio. Our conversation was interrupted by a phone call which I now know informed him of his father's death. At the time, I didn't know that.'

'What happened after the phone call?' Corbet continued.

'Well, I left and went into the studio and tried to get some rest. I knew that there was something eerie about the phone call, and that added to my unrest. I tried to sleep, dozed briefly and was awakened by the sound of an ambulance. There was a lot of movement in the hall outside my studio. I thought that it was probably Pierre, although what he was doing, I didn't know.

'When I got up to go downstairs and investigate, I ran into a strange young man who passed me in the hallway and went upstairs. I had never seen him before and haven't seen him since. I have no idea where he went when he got off of the elevator. I do know that somebody was still around the de La Roche apartment at that time. I just didn't see who it was.'

'And then what did you do?' Corbet pressed on.

'Well, when I got back to my studio, Gerard called me, and I told him about what had been going on. We talked for a while. He tried to comfort me. We made plans to meet the next day. That's about it. You know the rest from there.' Rachel sighed. Her weariness showed in her drawn face and dull eyes.

Corbet paid the bill and insisted on accompanying Rachel back to her apartment on the rue du Mont Thabor. Once inside, he glanced around the room. It was quite a contrast to the de La Roche quarters across the hall. The studio was one large, square room filled with great windows at least seven feet high, which opened on to a courtyard three floors down. The shutters were badly in need of paint. The building probably dated from the time of Napoleon, and the seedy elegance of the room itself suggested that it might not have been redecorated for at least fifty years.

The furnishings, probably antique, looked as though they could have been used by Balzac in the first half of the nineteenth century. Rachel's bed was a sofa, a daybed, covered with a somewhat faded, but once very elegant, green velveteen cover. There were water stains on the silk-grain wallpaper, and the floor was covered with a paltry brownish rug badly in need of a good cleaning.

Corbet escorted Rachel to a seat on the daybed. He thanked her for her help, wished her a good rest and recovery from recent events, and assured her that she would have the protection of his department until the case was solved.

He had to get to Valérie Ribeau and find out why she had suggested that Pierre accompany Rachel back from the monastery. Why she would exercise such poor judgement was a puzzle, and he needed an answer.

Chapter Twenty-Six

Place Victor Hugo was just beginning to flood with the afternoon-rush traffic as Corbet exited the Métro station. He reached the café where he was to meet Valérie and found her seated on a red velveteen banquette near a window dressed with white lace half-curtains on brass rods. She was smoking, and adjusted the ashtray and moved her glass of red wine as Corbet took a seat across from her. She did not meet his gaze.

'What would be good for a late lunch?' He opened with a neutral but pleasant topic.

'They have a good fish soup here. I usually get that when I want something light.' Valérie seemed glad to make small talk.

Corbet ordered the fish soup, another reminder of his early years in Provence. It came with a full accompaniment of garlic mayonnaise, cheese and croutons. Valérie continued to move the ashtray around the table, unable to find a place where she felt comfortable leaving it.

'I need to know why you recommended that Pierre bring Rachel back from Rouen. I need to know a lot about your relationship with Pierre.' There was no time to waste.

Valérie Ribeau took a deep drag on her cigarette and held the smoke for what seemed like a long time before she answered. Her hands were shaking, and she still avoided meeting Corbet's gaze.

'He threatened to have me fired if I didn't let him do it. He said he would tell Madame Bernard that I had helped him to perform some of his nefarious deeds, that I had been his accomplice. He didn't say what the deeds were, but from the way he looked and was acting it didn't take too much imagination to figure it out. I think he was involved in those murders. He was going to try to implicate me.' She paused and moved her shaking hand to her mouth to draw again on her cigarette.

'So, you sent him out to get Rachel Todd. Didn't you know you could have been risking her life by doing that? How could you have done it?' Corbet was exasperated with this wizened and desperate woman.

'He threatened me, I told you.'

'But if you really had nothing to do with these events, why did you let him intimidate you?' He would have his answer.

Valérie Ribeau gazed at him with a face full of frozen anxiety. She tried to explain to Corbet that she had reacted immediately to the threats of Pierre as though there were really something to them. All she was really guilty of was her association with him in the first place, the fact that she had used him as a contact for renting the studio, for providing housing for her students.

Her resentment and distrust of François de La Roche, her jealousy of Marie Marceau's relationship with Albert, all of these were real, but they were, after all, only feelings, not actions. She had reacted as though her negative feelings had convicted her of a crime.

'Well, you see, I had no great love for François de La Roche in the first place because of what happened to my sister. But I didn't kill him. I really didn't. I didn't even really know the other man, Albert. I knew Madame Marceau, his girlfriend, and she annoyed me. That's all.

'It was easier to deal with Pierre than to deal with Thérèse de La Roche. I tried to minimise my contact with her. It was too painful. I would always think about my sister.' Her eyes filled with tears as she crushed out her cigarette. She looked up at Corbet, who was not unmoved by her pain.

'My job is all I have. If I lose my job, there will be no one to look after me – no, that's not true. I do have my inherited money. But I would have no purpose without my job. I think I would just curl up and die somewhere without it.' Her eyes pleaded for understanding. Corbet gave it.

'Do you think he actually got to Madame Bernard with these allegations?'

'I don't know. She hasn't been in the office for a few days, and I imagine he couldn't reach her. I still don't trust him. He'll stop at nothing.' Her pinched face underlined her anxiety.

'It appears so,' Corbet responded. He was just finishing his fish soup, which he had managed to enjoy in spite of the tense conversation.

'I'll be in touch.' He paid the bill and left.

Chapter Twenty-Seven

When he arrived back at the Quai des Orfèvres, Corbet found Gilet pacing the hallway outside of his office and muttering to himself. As he turned to retrace his steps back for another pace, he almost banged into Corbet who had come up silently behind him.

'Am I glad to see you. Where have you been? Inspector Gautier from Bordeaux has been trying to reach you for hours.'

'Trying to tie up a lot of loose ends.' Corbet had backed away and was entering his office. He reached the desk, took out one of his chocolates, and popped it into his mouth as he turned to face Gilet, who now stood in the doorway.

'Well, we've got loose ends here. Flagon still hasn't told Gautier who his accomplice is. Says he needs to talk to you, that he has some important information for you on the other prints. You're to call him as soon as you get in.'

'Well, let me do it then.' Corbet got up to close the door and make the necessary telephone call to Bordeaux. He picked up the phone and dialled the number of Inspector Gautier. After the initial 'hello's, he got right to the point. Apparently Inspector Gautier and his men were still working on identifying the partial print on the container. It was really just a fragment and was causing them some trouble, but he wanted Corbet to know they were close to making a match. Corbet sighed and hung up the phone. Apprehending the killer would just take longer. That was all there was to it. He vowed to persist.

Chapter Twenty-Eight

Corbet escorted Marie into the main dining-room of La Tour d'Argent. He knew she would be pleased by the understated elegance of the decor, the Louis XV chairs in pale green, the yards of white damask table cloths, the antique silver and the Limoges. The maître d' led them to a table for two in the back of the restaurant, right in the window, overlooking the splendour of Notre Dame. The candlelight in the room complemented the lights along the Quai de la Tournelle and those which illuminated the back of the grand old dame, exposing her buttresses and solid grace.

As she took her seat, Marie smiled a warm and grateful smile. She took Corbet's hand. 'Thank you for this lovely idea.'

Corbet could feel his heart begin to beat faster, and he felt as awkward as a teenager on his first date. This was, after all, like a first date. His dream was shattered by his remembering what he had to tell Marie this evening. It hadn't occurred to him that the romance of the setting might make it more difficult for him to tell her. He had only thought of how she would enjoy this and how he would enjoy a go at the duck and a brief reprieve from the complications of the case at hand.

'Yes, I hear the duck is not to be missed. Funny, I've always meant to come here but never really have. I guess it's not really the sort of restaurant one goes to alone.' Corbet took the wine list from the waiter and began to examine it. His eye passed over the Margaux, and he thought of Bordeaux and Thérèse and what he had to tell Marie. He ordered Châteauneuf-du-Pape which he thought might be particularly good with the duck. Marie agreed.

She looked beautiful in an apricot-coloured suit with a white silk blouse. Her face was beginning to light up and lose some of the drawn look she had had at their last meeting. The place was obviously agreeing with her. Corbet was pleased. The purpose of his mission needled him, but it could wait just a bit.

He combed the menu out of curiosity. His decision to have the duck had been made before he entered the restaurant. Marie hesitated between the duck and chicken with truffles. Corbet filed the idea of those luscious, little black fungi combined with a plump chicken away for future experimentation in his own kitchen. Marie decided she would go with the duck, too. It was to be accompanied by a purée of white turnip and leeks, a combination which quite intrigued Corbet. There would also be a version of Potatoes Anna, a dish of sliced potatoes layered and baked with duck fat. Corbet's mouth watered at the prospect.

Two apéritifs were brought to the table. Corbet began to sip his. He looked at Marie. His eyes responded to her loveliness first with unabashed appreciation, and then he lowered his lids with sorrowful regret as he remembered what he must tell her. Maybe he could wait until another time, maybe after the gathering at Thérèse de La Roche's.

'How are you doing?' Corbet took her hand and waited for her reply.

'I think I'm better. The pain is still with me, of course, but I've begun to sleep a little. I still feel haunted and won't really rest until we have an answer as to who killed him. You see, I still can't believe that somebody actually killed him in cold blood. Seems impossible to me. We had been

152

planning a trip to Illiers/Combray; in fact, it was for next week. We still have the reservations. I think I'll go out there myself and just get some rest.'

'Do you really think that's wise? Won't it be too painful?' The waiter cleared the plates from the soup course and began the elaborate business of serving the duck, and Corbet had to wait for his answer. The aroma of the cooked creatures and the accompanying vegetables distracted him further. He might be able to enjoy the duck, but there was no way he was going to be able to avoid telling Marie of his discovery about Albert. That was all there was to it. At least the duck remained. He took his first delightful forkful and repeated his question.

'Do you really think that's wise?'

'Oh, Henri, this is truly divine. And the vegetables are exquisite.' She looked at Corbet with unguarded admiration.

The joy that look produced in him, along with the flavour of the duck and vegetables, almost convinced him that he might wait with the news.

Marie continued. 'But, no, I really think I'll be fine. It may really help me come to terms with what has happened. If it's too painful, I can come home. Besides, I want to learn more about Proust myself. Roger has some students whom I know it would help if they could meet with me to discuss their ongoing projects. I feel I ought to help out at least that much.' Marie continued to savour her duck.

'But surely there are other colleagues of his who can take over that responsibility?'

'Well, there probably are, but I want to do it. I need to do it.'

'If you must, you must.' The tartness of the turnip and leek purée helped to push Corbet's attention back to his mission. He would wait at least until dessert.

The Châteauneuf-du-Pape was adding a mellow round-ness to the meal, and he didn't want to spoil it now. They made small-talk about the setting and the food for the rest of the meal. When the waiter cleared the plates and brought the dessert card, Corbet knew he must begin to mobilise. The apple tart seemed a good choice, not only to comple-ment the meal, but also to help move him with his mission.

'Marie, there's something I must tell you. I've been de-bating with myself all evening about whether I could wait and tell you later, but I've decided I must tell you now, because I need to see if it will give me any further answers to the riddle of these murders.' Corbet took his first bite of apple tart.

'Why, of course, Henri. Do tell me.' Marie gazed at him with intense curiosity, her forkful of apple tart poised midway between her plate and her mouth.

'I remember your telling me that Albert had been very preoccupied before his death and that you had at first suspected that he might be involved with another woman.' Corbet eyed her intently.

'Yes, I did tell you that, and I did think it for a while.' She took her second bite of the apple tart and waited.

Corbet looked at her, his eyes filled with warmth and compassion, and he wished that he could spare her this news. The bite of tart he was chewing stuck to the back of his throat as he tried to get the words out. He took a drink of his coffee to wash it down.

'Well, I have it from a pretty reliable source that your initial instincts were correct, that indeed Albert was involved with another woman, and that woman was Thérèse de La Roche.' Corbet didn't dare go near the tart again.

'But that can't be. He...' Marie's eyes filled with tears. She lowered her head and seemed to stare at the remainder of the tart on her plate without really seeing it.

'He…' She began to sob softly. Corbet reached over, took her hand and wished he could be anywhere but here telling her this news. He would rather have been swimming in the Seine or scaling the ribs of Notre Dame like Quasimodo, anything but doing this.

'How could he, with that woman?' Marie asked the question of the half-empty plate. It had no answer, but Corbet did. He could understand how he could, but he couldn't tell Marie that. She would never understand. 'What about François de La Roche? I thought he was such a good friend of his.' Marie eyed Corbet and waited for an answer.

'Yes, that must have been very difficult for him. From what I can gather, he was genuinely fond of François de La Roche. He must have suffered some conflict over that.' Corbet disliked becoming the defender of Albert, but indeed this must have been the truth. He didn't envy his being in the middle of so much emotional turmoil. He wondered whether Albert's infatuation with Thérèse de La Roche had convinced him that he no longer loved Marie. If so, that would have been yet another source of intense conflict. No wonder the man seemed preoccupied.

'But how could he?' This was all Marie could manage through her tears. Corbet couldn't give her the answer. He took her hand.

'I don't know,' he lied. 'But he did, and now we must deal with what that might mean. The girlfriend of René Simon, Jacqueline Champigneulle, told me that both Simon and Albert were very taken with Thérèse de La Roche. She also told me that they were both being pursued by Pierre, the son of François de La Roche. Did Albert ever mention anything about Pierre?' He continued to hold her hand. She began to compose herself and to think about his question.

'Now that you mention it, yes. Roger told me that Pierre seemed to lurk about a lot when he was visiting with François in the apartment in Paris. He said that he was always overly solicitous to him and that this made him uncomfortable. He even felt that sometimes he was flirting with him. I never took too much notice of it. There are many eccentric characters in Paris, and I figured this was just another one. We are used to it.'

He hesitated to get to the hard part, but he knew he had to. 'Before you had dinner with Albert at La Semaine, before he was killed, do you know where he was earlier that evening or even during the day?' Corbet eyed Marie's half-empty plate and waited for an answer.

'Why, Henri, you don't think that – you can't think that Roger could have had anything to do with the death of de La Roche?' Her eyes filled with tears, and they began to run slowly down her cheeks.

Corbet felt his heart twist at her pain, but he had to persist. 'I know this is difficult, Marie. I know, but I need to find out. I need to cover all of the angles. That's my job. We really do want get to the bottom of this, don't we?' He gazed at her softly.

'Yes, we do.' She wiped her tears with her damask napkin and took a sip of her coffee. 'We have to. I really don't know where Roger was before he came to my apartment in the evening to have dinner. I had expected to hear from him earlier in the day but didn't.'

'Would his involvement with Thérèse de La Roche have been enough to make him want François dead? That's the question we must answer.' Corbet continued to gaze softly at Marie.

'You know, Henri, I'm shocked to learn that Roger was involved with her, but I don't honestly believe that he would kill anybody, even if he were madly obsessed with love. I just don't think he would be capable of it. I'm sure that he suffered a great deal with the complications of the situation. It was a very haunted man that I lived with at the end.' She seemed to rise above her pain and shock and come to Albert's defence.

Corbet was not surprised. Her nature was loyal and loving. Albert had been a lucky man.

'No, I don't really believe he was involved in it, either, but I had to bring it up with you in case in some way it might jog your memory.'

He did not tell her just how far he was on the road to solving at least the murder of de La Roche, if not the other two. It would be a long night.

On the whole, however, he was glad for the respite provided by the duck, the view of Notre Dame, and the company of Marie, even under these circumstances. The last swallow of the Châteauneuf-du-Pape brought his thoughts to his upcoming encounter with Thérèse de La Roche. He had a lot to discuss with her. He hoped it wouldn't be too late. He saw Marie home in a cab and headed back to the Quai des Orfèvres.

Chapter Twenty-Nine

Gilet was waiting for him when he arrived back at the Préfecture. He assured him that the surveillance on 37 rue du Mont Thabor was very tight indeed and that nothing out of the ordinary had been observed there.

Corbet settled back in his chair. The duck and the Châteauneuf-du-Pape were digesting well and gave him a slight cushion against the distress of the situation at hand. He felt quite certain that Marie would recover and that her knowledge of the truth would help in her healing. She was a delicate but strong woman. His instinct had been right about telling her. The good feelings about the mission accomplished helped to buoy him on towards the closure he sought in the cases.

The thought of the encounter with Thérèse de La Roche was troubling. He dialled her number and she answered, sounding sleepy and distracted. He pleaded with her for an interview tonight or at least early tomorrow. She resisted at first, but when he pressed she agreed to meet him in the bar of the Hotel Lotti. It was close to her apartment, and she wouldn't have to disturb Pierre with a late-night visitor. Corbet agreed to meet her there in an hour. It was now 11.30 p.m. The bar didn't close until 1 a.m.

He pulled his solid form out of the cab and entered the lobby of the Hotel Lotti. He remembered that he had once eaten in the delightful restaurant with his mother and father many years ago. A memory of New Year's goose surfaced. There had been an unusual Central European cabbage and apple stuffing. He remembered his father saying that the chef was from Vienna.

He ordered an Armagnac and waited for Thérèse to arrive. The meal and the evening with Marie were still with him, and he felt well anchored for what might prove to be a difficult encounter. He saw her enter the bar from across the room. She was dressed entirely in black – black coat, sweater and long skirt. Her hair was swept back, and she looked stunning.

As she approached the table where Corbet sat, he noticed an air of fatigue around her eyes and that she wasn't wearing much make-up. But she was still beautiful, in any case. Corbet caught his breath as she approached. He felt his heart begin to beat faster. He clutched his glass of Armagnac, wishing he dared to take a big swill. Instead he offered her a seat and motioned for the waiter. She ordered a brandy. The waiter brought her drink, and she sat clutching the large snifter and waiting for Corbet to begin. He did, but gently.

'It's good to see you again, Madame de La Roche.' Now he took a large swill of his Armagnac.

'Yes, I suppose it is. I'll be glad when this dreadful business is over. So many things are happening so fast. Poor François is not even buried yet.' She stared numbly off into space.

'Well, that's why I wanted to see you tonight, so we can begin to get some closure on these events. I'm sorry about the timing, but I must ask you some questions.' Corbet's eyes pleaded with her for understanding.

'I know. It's just that – well, this is difficult.' She seemed to be genuinely distressed, not at all that cool woman he had interviewed down at the château. Could it be that she was just coming to terms with the fact that her husband had been murdered, or did it have to do with Albert? Maybe it was an act.

'I know this hasn't been pleasant, to say the least. But I must persist. I know you understand.' He looked at her and waited for her response.

'I do. Ask what you need to ask.' She waited for the questions like a martyr waiting for her execution, with patience and deference.

'Jacqueline Champigneulle told me about your relationship with Roger Albert.' He dropped the news in her lap and waited for her reaction.

'Yes, I'm sure she did. It was getting really very complicated at the end. Simon was being such a pest. He was like a dog with a bone with the news of my relationship with Roger. He was prone to all sorts of urbane affectations, but he seemed genuinely disturbed by this. For me it had been over a long time ago with him and would have been even if I hadn't found out about his father's activities during the war. You know that his father was one of the worst collaborators in the Vichy government?' She eyed Corbet somewhat coldly.

'Yes, I know that.' Corbet took a swig of his Armagnac.

'I always felt it was just his ego, that because I had been the one to call it quits, he needed to win me back again in order to cut the cord himself. Maybe I was wrong. At any rate, he was obsessed with me. He didn't take the news of my relationship with Roger very well.'

'When did he find out?' The timing of this was very important to Corbet. He waited.

'Oh, I think it was just shortly before François was killed. Maybe about a week, something like that, maybe two weeks. I know I saw him in Paris before I went down to the château for the grape harvest. He was chewing on it then.' She took a long sip of her brandy and put her head back and closed her eyes. Corbet eyed her long and graceful throat.

'Did he make any threats or anything of that nature?' Corbet waited.

'No, not really. Nothing direct, but I felt somehow that he could be dangerous. He made me very uncomfortable. I was very, very concerned about François and how he would take it if he found out about it. He had always had the habit of looking the other way from my amusements, but this one was a little close to home. He was truly fond of Albert, treated him like the son he had never found in Pierre. It would have broken his heart to know about this. I felt we shouldn't tell him. Roger was very tormented about it. He, too, was very fond of François. He was also afraid of Pierre, who apparently had been pestering him for a while, seeking his favours. Of course you know about Pierre?' She gazed directly at Corbet and waited.

'I know that he's rather unstable and that he prefers men to women, if that's what you mean.'

'That's what I mean,' she continued. 'There was no telling how he would react. However, I felt that we should tell him to prevent his assaulting François with the news. I felt I still held enough sway with him to get him to promise me not to tell François. Roger was not so sure.'

'And then there was the problem of Marie. He had been with her for some time and genuinely cared for her. What was between us was just one of those irresistible passions. Thank goodness they don't happen very often. In all honesty, I was very taken with him, too.' She lowered her eyes and sighed. Tears began to stream down her cheeks. 'I really miss him. It had been years since anyone had touched me.'

Corbet was moved by her sadness, but he did not take her hand. He only waited for her to regain her composure. He thought it odd that he was comforting two women to whom he was very attracted, both of whom had been in love with Roger Albert. The pang of jealousy he felt was not washed away with the next big swig of Armagnac.

Thérèse was still irresistible to him, and he was very fond of Marie. He continued to wait.

'I didn't tell Pierre. Then I got the news about François's death, and then that of Roger. When I spoke with you at the château, I didn't know about Roger's death. I only learned about it the day you left. Otherwise, I'm sure I would have been much more upset than I was. Of course I was upset about François, but we had lived at such an emotional distance for so long that it wasn't the kind of crushing blow that the news about Roger was. You can understand that?'

'Of course,' Corbet replied, and in spite of himself, he could. However, he needed to continue. 'Can you tell me when you discovered your husband's connection with the Vichy government? Did you know that when you married him?'

Thérèse de La Roche seemed surprised and caught off guard by the question. 'Why, no, as a matter of fact, I didn't know about it. I didn't marry François because I loved him, you know?' She eyed Corbet coldly.

'I gathered that.' Corbet stared back.

'He represented some form of security and protection. I lost a lot during the war.' Her voice trailed off, and she seemed to stare into space.

'I've heard about your father.' Corbet waited.

She sat silently for some time, and then took a large swig of her drink. 'He was a very good man. I never got over it. My heart shut down after that happened. Survival became my only goal. I probably wasn't a very good mother to Pierre, although he meant the world to me. I feel I've let him down somehow. He sets such store by the fact that he has an aristocratic background, but I'm afraid he's much like those with such a background who suffer from too much inbreeding.' The coolness of her assessment of her son intrigued Corbet.

'What about the connection between Albert and Gerard Goode? What do you know about that?'

'Well, I know that Roger was trying to reunite François with Gerard. He was François's first son from his marriage to Hélène. I guess you know that he had been sent to England by the Germans, with the help of François, during the war?'

'Yes, I knew that.' Corbet waited for her to continue.

'I knew that François really wanted to make amends to Gerard before he died. He was obsessed with that. We had no idea how far he might go with it.' Thérèse continued to stare somewhat blankly at the floor.

'Actually, even though I never said it to him, I thought that part of Roger's motivation to reunite François with Gerard was his guilt about his relationship with me and the fact that François seemed to treat him like a son. Maybe he thought it would be easier for him to bear the news of our relationship if he had his own real son back.' She lowered her eyes and took another large sip of her brandy.

'It makes sense.' Corbet took the last swig of his Armagnac and put the glass squarely on the table. He gazed at Thérèse, who seemed more relaxed but looked very tired. 'I know this has been hard on you. I want to thank you very much for meeting me here tonight at this hour. You've been helpful.'

'Why, of course, Inspector. It's the least I can do. I do want this whole ordeal to be over. You will come tomorrow?' Her eyes seemed to plead with him.

'Of course I will. Now go and get some rest.' He escorted her to the door and tried to put her in a cab, but she insisted on walking the short distance around the corner to her apartment and would not hear of his walking with her. He would head home and check with the Préfecture by phone.

Chapter Thirty

Corbet waited in the hall of 37 rue du Mont Thabor for the elevator so he could ascend to the de La Roche apartment. At the apartment door he was met by a man dressed in black tails who bowed to him as he entered and offered to take his coat. The large drawing-room was filled with about a hundred people, all of whom had had some connection to François and had come to say a last farewell and to offer support to his widow.

The room was brightly lit from the chandeliers above as well as lamps below. Along the wall across from the large marble fireplace with the gilt mirror was a large table covered with white damask and spread with the most tempting of morsels.

Corbet quickly noted that it was a delightful combination of a French luncheon and an English tea. His eye followed the table from left to right. On the far left end there was an elegant display of mousses and pâtés: salmon mousse, chicken liver pâté, pâté de campagne, pâté de foie gras with truffles, then a large basket of freshly baked rolls and baguettes, a magnificent cheese plate filled with everything from goat cheese to roquefort, and finally a plate of madeleines. At the end of the French luncheon items there was a large group of bottles of wine from the de La Roche vineyards, reds and whites, and a good supply of champagne.

The next grouping of food further to the right was the English spread of cucumber sandwiches, scones, clotted cream and a panoply of preserves. The right end of the table was flanked with large silver tea services and many Limoges cups and saucers and buffet plates.

Corbet had to check himself from making a beeline to this table of bounty which seemed as yet untouched. The butlers were bringing around glasses of sherry on trays, and he quickly took one. A group of very distinguished-looking gentlemen had gathered at the marble fireplace, apparently waiting for the ceremony to begin.

The first speech was given by François's closest friend, a former French ambassador to England and Austria. His high praise for François's talent and his struggle to come to terms with his past was eloquent and moving.

During the short speeches of the other dignitaries present, Corbet allowed his eye to wander around the room and noticed that Pierre was moving in and out of the people, having little tête-à-tête conversations with many of them. In the room right next to the drawing-room, he noticed the presence of Valérie Ribeau and Rachel Todd, who were seated together along the wall. They didn't seem to be talking to one another. He scanned the room for Marie. He had hoped that she would come, but was unsure just how the news of Albert's relationship with Thérèse was settling. He couldn't find her.

When the dignitaries had finished their eulogies, it was Simon's turn to say something. He took centre stage as though it had been made for him and began to praise François for his talent as a writer and his importance as a chronicler of our times. He seemed, as usual, cool and self-assured. However, from time to time he kept glancing in the direction of Thérèse as if to reassure himself that she was listening to what he was saying. The end of his speech was the signal to approach the food table.

A line formed, and Corbet took his place in it, eager to sample the spread. With a plate full of salmon mousse, pâté de foie gras with truffles and cucumber sandwiches, Corbet sought a chair along the wall of the next room. He had just set about the business of enjoying his little cucumber sandwiches when the butler escorted Marie in, and she took a seat beside him.

'This is probably about the best thing in the English cuisine, if you can really call it a cuisine,' he said savouring his morsel.

'Oh, yes, I like those, too,' Marie said in a strong voice.

'I'm very glad you came.' Corbet smiled at her. 'But do go help yourself to the feast.' Marie made her way to the table.

As he sat there savouring the treasures on his plate, Corbet glanced up to see Gilet heading toward him with a look of mission on his face. He bent over and whispered into Corbet's ear and handed him a paper. Inspector Gautier had made the match of the partial print. Corbet's suspicions were confirmed. He nodded a thank-you at Gilet who left the room as quickly as he had entered.

Corbet looked around the room and noticed that Pierre, who had been circulating among the people, was now engaged in what appeared to be a very intense conversation with Simon in a far corner of the room. He was unable to overhear what they were saying. He did notice, however, that both seemed very involved in the discussion. Thérèse was over in the other corner with her husband's friends.

When Marie returned from the buffet, he continued to make small-talk with her while he kept Pierre under surveillance. In the mill and mix of people positions shifted, and Thérèse and Simon were now in front of the large fireplace in what appeared to be deep conversation.

Pierre was over at the tea service and then turned to approach them, holding two Limoges cups and saucers in his hand. When he greeted Thérèse and Simon, he handed each of them a cup. Each took it with a smile of thanks. He stood by and tried to engage them in conversation.

Simon kept shifting his glance from Pierre to Thérèse. Just as she was about to put the cup of tea to her lips, Simon knocked it out of her hand with a broad sweep of his large hand and forearm. He then raised his own cup to his mouth. Almost instantaneously, Corbet lunged across the room and knocked Simon's cup out of his hand before it reached his lips. The double crash of the Limoges breaking on the fireplace tiles acted like an alarm, drawing the attention of many in the room to the area. Thérèse looked at Simon and Corbet with a puzzled, shocked expression.

By now people were milling actively in the room. The butler was trying to clean up the pieces of Limoges. Thérèse sought refuge in a seat along the wall. Simon continued to stand by the fireplace. Corbet headed straight for the phone and called his men who had been on standby in Rachel's studio. Within a minute, they were in the de La Roche apartment. Two of them went for Pierre who let them apprehend him without much of a struggle. He was babbling something about his mother and how she had betrayed him.

Two more officers were trying to keep order in the group. People were gathering around in shock and horror. Pierre was led out of the apartment with his hands cuffed behind his back. Thérèse sat in her chair along the wall of the drawing-room, tears streaming down her face. Once Corbet had seen to the operations of his men, he approached and took a seat next to her.

'Maybe it will end now.' Her eyes pleaded with him.

'We can hope it will, Madame,' was all he could manage to say.

Chapter Thirty-One

Corbet snuggled his solid form into a booth at the Jockey and waited for Marie. There were no students today. In fact, they might almost have the place to themselves. He quickly noted that the plat du jour was eggs florentine, one of his favourites. Marie approached the booth and seated herself across from him. He took her hand and smiled at her.

'At least we've gotten to the bottom of it now?' His eyes inquired of her.

'Yes. I'm thankful for that. The pain is still with me, but knowing the truth does make it easier to deal with it. I'm glad you didn't spare me, Henri.' She squeezed his hand and released hers from his grip as she took the menu from the waiter. They agreed on the eggs florentine and a bottle of Vouvray.

'But you must tell me how you sorted it all out, Henri.' Marie waited.

Corbet told her about Pierre's confession after his arrest, about that of Jules Flagon, who evidently liked both men and women and had at one time been Pierre's lover. He pointed out that even without the Flagon confession, all hands had pointed to either Thérèse or Pierre de La Roche, and that the match of the partial fingerprint from the cyanide container had provided the hard evidence.

'Pierre said that he had killed de La Roche to avenge his grandfather d'Aubery's murder by the Vichy government, as well as to ensure that Gerard Goode didn't inherit what Pierre felt was his rightful share of the de La Roche estate.

'It seems that Pierre was lost in some fantasy about winning a power struggle to head the family as the rightful heir of François's estate. Thus, at the scene of François's murder, Pierre had his hired killer, Flagon, put the cyanide in the artificial sweetener in the monogrammed pillbox, and the madeleines were wrapped in a napkin bearing the family coat of arms.

'In each instance, he had entry to the restaurants where Marie and Albert and, then, Rachel Todd and Gerard were the only customers. He simply placed the cyanide in the tea, they drank it, and that killed them.

'He had intended to kill Rachel Todd, too, but she hadn't drunk the tea yet. As for Simon, he was beginning to come apart. He was distressed and put off by the degree of Pierre's obsession. They were in cahoots on the murder of François. We have that from Pierre. However, beyond that, it appears that Simon wanted out of the deal once he saw the degree of Pierre's disturbance. Pierre then began to act on his own, killing Albert and Goode.'

'Why the use of poison?' Marie seemed fascinated by Corbet's comments.

'Good of you to pick that up. The use of poison itself was a clue in the solution of the murders. Thérèse had been poisoned with hatred and resentment towards de La Roche whom she somehow blamed for the death of her father, although certainly Simon's father probably had more to do with it than de La Roche. She in turn became very cold to de La Roche, and turned all her attention and venom on Pierre. She literally poisoned him, his thinking, taking advantage of an already distant and unloving relationship between him and his father. Pierre, in his attempt to rescue his mother, establish his own power and oust the pretenders, committed the murders by a literal poisoning of the victims.

'Simon became involved as an accomplice because he wanted de La Roche out of the way so that the publication of the book could proceed as he saw fit without opposition from de La Roche. What he didn't count on was that with his background, even if Thérèse de La Roche were madly in love with him, she would feel compelled to hate him and seek vengeance because of his father's nefarious deeds during the war. He couldn't win with her. To get back at her, he told Pierre about her relationship with Albert, knowing that it would fracture him. It added fuel to the fire and gave Pierre more reason to murder Albert. Pierre said he couldn't stop himself. He felt very betrayed by his mother because of her relationship with Albert, the man who was trying to bring de La Roche together with his first son.

'In his desperation and anger, Pierre tried to kill his mother and Simon. Simon's withdrawal as an accomplice and his involvement with Thérèse could hardly have endeared him to Pierre. Simon rescued Thérèse only to try to kill himself. He must have figured the jig would be up for him once his father's connections with Vichy became known, and I guess he was despondent over his inability to win the heart of Thérèse de La Roche. What a tangled web we weave.'

'So the real murderer goes free?' Marie looked very sad and gave a sigh of resignation.

'I guess you could say that. Where does the chain stop?' Corbet stared off into space and wondered what Thérèse de La Roche's life would be like now, whether her urge for vengeance had been satisfied, if the price had been too high.'

'And the madeleines?'

'Well, they were the little titbit that led Proust back to his childhood to rediscover many memories. Perhaps Pierre was trying to get back to his, a time when he thought he was the only thing in his mother's life. They also carry a sexual symbolism. The shape of the round shell suggests a feminine form, thus Pierre's sexual confusion and strong attachment to his mother.' Corbet glanced at Marie, who raised her eyebrows at this suggestion.

'Then there is the idea of how we carry our past embedded in us, even if we can't readily feel or see it.' Corbet drained his glass of Vouvray and dove into the elegant eggs florentine.

Epilogue

The train pulled out of the Gare Saint Lazare and headed in the direction of Rouen. Corbet snuggled down in his seat with his paperback copy of *Le Rouge et le noir*. A couple of days out at the Abbey of Saint Wandrille would calm his soul after his recent encounter with death and deception. Then it was on to Cabourg and the elegant Grand Hotel on the Atlantic where Proust had gone so often to write.

Inspector Henri Corbet was positive that some time spent walking the beach and breathing the sea air would go far in restoring him. The distinguished menu in the elegant dining-room would also make its contribution. Maybe he would finish his book on the Russian campaign of Napoleon. He looked forward to reading the *Memoirs of François de La Roche* which Galliante had agreed to publish posthumously and unaltered.